CHRONICLES OF AN ESCAPADE

BY: NAHBEEL RICHARDSON

Chapter 1

ALL TOO FAMILIAR AND TRUE, IS THE SAYING, "ALL BEGINNINGS, HAVE SIMILAR ENDS," MY SIMILARITY BEING A MEDICAL SETTING, WITH THE ONLY DIFFERENCE BEING HOW I WENT FROM A ROUTINE DENTIST VISIT, TO BEING HOSPITALIZED. WELL, I GUESS I SHOULD EXPLAIN.

IT WAS AN EARLY MORNING IN APRIL WHEN I AWOKE WITH A POUNDING IN MY HEAD SO INTENSE, ANY SLIGHT MOVEMENT, SOUND, OR LIGHT WAS GIVING MY NERVES AS MUCH PAIN AS A 10.0 EARTHQUAKE DOES TO BUILDINGS. YEAH, THAT BAD. WITH AS MUCH STRENGTH AS I COULD MUSTER, I IMMEDIATELY CALLED MY DENTIST. BEING AS THOUGH IT WAS AN EMERGENCY, HE

TOLD ME TO COME IN AS SOON AS POSSIBLE. I, THEN, CALLED IN SICK TO MY JOB, THANKING GOD I STILL HAD A DAY TO TAKE OFF. FOR A MOMENT AFTERWARDS, I JUST HAD TO LIE THERE, PRAYING THE PAIN WOULD SUBSIDE LONG ENOUGH, TO WHERE I COULD ACTUALLY MAKE IT TO THE DENTIST.

AFTER I COULD NO LONGER TAKE THE PAIN OF MY TOOTHACHE, I GET UP AND SHOWER. WITH A SIMPLE PLUSH TOWEL WRAPPED AROUND MY BREAST I STAND IN FRONT OF MY CLOSET NOT KNOWING WHAT TO WEAR. I HEAR THE FRONT DOOR SLAM CLOSE AND THE VIBRATIONS SEEM TO INCREASE MY PAIN. NO LONGER CARING WHAT I WEAR, I JUST START PULLING ANYTHING OUT.

I TURN AROUND FROM PLACING MY OUTFIT ON MY BED TO THE OPENING OF MY BEDROOM DOOR. "DAMN BOY, DON'T YOU KNOW HOW TO KNOCK?!"

"GIRL, PLEASE. AIN'T NO KNOCKING IN THIS HOUSE. BESIDES, YOU DON'T GOT NOTHING I HAVEN'T SEEN ALREADY."

"WELL, YOU AIN'T SEEING THIS. GET OUT." I BEGIN TO GET DRESSED BY PULLING UP MY PANTIES UNDERNEATH MY TOWEL.

THE YOUNGER OF MY TWO OLDER BROTHERS, SALEEM, SITS ON MY BED. "YO, WHY DO BITCHES DO THE SHIT THEY DO, MAN?"

"'LEEM, GET-OUT."

"COME ON, YANI. I NEED TO TALK," HE WHINES.

"NOT TO ME, YOU DON'T."

"WHY NOT?" HE ASKS. "FUCK WRONG WITH YOU? WE ALWAYS TALK."

"FIRST AND FOREMOST," I SAY WIGGLING INTO MY JEANS. "I'M NOT A BITCH."

"SHIT, YANI. COME ON WITH THAT BEING SMART SHIT. YOU KNOW WHAT I MEAN."

"AND SECONDLY, I'M ON MY WAY TO THE DENTIST. I HAD TO CALL OFF FROM WORK TODAY, MY MOUTH HURTS SO BAD."

LEEM TAKES A MOMENT OF SILENCE, AND THEN LOOKS AT ME PUZZLED. HEAD COCKED TO THE SIDE, HE ASKS, "WHAT YOU GOT A TOOTHACHE?"

YES, I KNOW, GENIUS. WHAT CAN I TELL YOU? IF THEY MADE HALVES OF A CENT, I WOULD GIVE HIM ONE, JUST SO HE COULD HAVE TWO. THAT'S MY BROTHER. "YES, LEEM," I SIGH.

"WHAT YOU SAY IT LIKE THAT FOR?!" HE ASKS DEFENSIVELY. "LIKE YOU GOT AN ATTITUDE OR SOMETHING. CAN'T EVEN SHOW NO LOVE TO NO BITCH, MAN. THAT'S CRAZY."

I PULL MY SHIRT OVER MY HEAD AND SIT DOWN IN FRONT OF MY VANITY. I LET MY ELECTRONIC HOT COMB BEGIN TO WARM AS I START ON MY MAKE UP. "I TOLD YOU BOUT CALLING ME A BITCH," I WARN HIM.

LEEM SUCKS HIS TEETH.

WITH A SIGH, SEEING AS THOUGH I HAVE TO GET FINISHED GETTING READY, I DECIDE TO HELP HIM WITH ONE OF HIS MANY CRISES, WHICH IT SEEMS LIKE I'M THE ONLY ONE HE CONFIDES IN. IT SHOULD BE THE OTHER WAY AROUND, BEING AS THOUGH I'M THE BABY. SOMETIMES I THINK THAT BEING FOURTEEN MONTHS APART AND GROWING UP AS CLOSE AS WE DID, WHERE WE COULD ALWAYS TALK ABOUT ANYTHING AND EVERYTHING AT ANY GIVEN TIME, IS A CURSE.

"WHAT HAPPENED?" I INEVITABLY ASK.

"TOYA LEFT ME," LEEM EXPLAINS.

"WHAT? SHE LEFT YOU? WHY?"

"I DON'T KNOW."

MORE

I TURN AROUND TO FACE HIM. "YOU DON'T KNOW?"

"THAT'S WHAT I SAID, AIN'T IT?"

"YOU DIDN'T ASK WHY?"

"NAW, SHE SAID SHE NEEDS A BREAK. ALWAYS KNEW THAT BITCH WAS NO GOOD. PROBABLY GIVING MY SHIT UP TO ANOTHER NIGGA RIGHT NOW."

"PUMP YA BRAKES FOR A MINUTE, SALEEM. JUST BECAUSE SHE SAID NEEDS 'A BREAK', DOESN'T MEAN SHE LEFT YOU OR THAT SHE'S GETTING IT IN WITH ANOTHER DUDE."

"WHAT THEN? EXPLAIN IT TO ME."

"ARE YOU GOING TO BE QUIET LONG ENOUGH FOR ME TO TALK; BECAUSE IF NOT, YOU CAN HANDLE IT ON YOUR OWN AND SEE HOW FAR THAT'LL GET YOU."

"AIGHT, GO HEAD." AND HE LAYS BACK ON MY BED, AS IF HE'S IN A PSYCHIATRIST OFFICE OR SOMETHING.

MORE

"WHAT HAPPENED JUST BEFORE SHE SAID THAT SHE NEEDED 'A BREAK'?"

"I LAID THE PIPE," HE SAYS PROUDLY.

"AFTER THAT," I PROBE AND FINALLY, WE GET TO THE ROOT OF THE PROBLEM.

"WE WERE ARGUING 'BOUT SOMETHING."

"ABOUT… WHAT?"

"MAN, I DON'T KNOW. ASK HER," HE SAYS WITH AN ATTITUDE.

"SO, YOU DON'T KNOW WHY YOU WERE ARGUING, YOU WERE JUST ARGUING FOR THE SAKE OF ARGUING?"

"WHAT? WAIT, LET ME THINK." HE PAUSES FOR A MOMENT, THEN,

"SHE WAS TRYING TO TELL ME SOMETHING. TELL ME SHE

HAD TO DO

SOMETHING? OR WANTED ME TO DO SOMETHING FOR

HER? SOMETHING MAN, I

DON'T KNOW."

"HEY LEEM, WHAT ARE YOU DOING TODAY?"

HE LEANS UP ON AN ELBOW. "NOTHING WHY

WHAT'S UP?"

"YOU SEE HOW QUICK YOU JUMPED TO HELP ME

WITH SOMETHING AND

YOU DIDN'T EVEN KNOW WHAT IT WAS?"

"YEAH…, SO?"

"THAT'S WHAT TOYA WANTS FROM YOU."

"HUNH? NAW, MAN. THAT'S DIFFERENT."

"WHY? BECAUSE I'M YOUR SISTER AND SHE'S YOUR

GIRL?"

"EXACTLY," HE AGREES EXCITEDLY, AS I QUICKLY CAUGHT HIS MEANING.

"WHAT'S THE DIFFERENCE?" I ASK OUT OF CURIOSITY.

"BECAUSE I'M BANGING HER AND NOT YOU."

"SO, JUST BECAUSE YOU 'BANGING' A CHICK WHO SUPPOSE TO BE YOUR GIRL, MEANS YOU CAN'T DO ANYTHING FOR HER?"

"I GUESS. I DON'T KNOW, MAN. ALL I KNOW IS THAT I AIN'T FEELING LIKE DOING IT, OK?"

"MM-MM-MM. CALL HER LEEM."

"NAW, I AIN'T DOING THAT."

"WHY ARE YOU BEING SELFISH?" I ASK.

"I AIN'T SELFISH. I WAS TIRED. SHE SHOULDA ASKED ME BEFORE I BUST."

"SO, YOU GOT WHAT YOU WANTED, BUT SHE CAN'T?"

"OH, SHE DEFINITELY GOT WHAT SHE WANTED." AND HE LAUGHS.

"OH, BOY YOU NASTY. NOW DO YOU WANT MY ADVICE OR NOT?" AFTER NOT GETTING A RESPONSE, I CONTINUE. "CALL TOYA UP AND APOLOGIZE."

"WHAT? I YANI I AIN'T APOLOGIZING FOR SHIT. I AIN'T DONE NOTHING."

"APOLOGIZE FOR THE SAKE OF APOLOGIZING THEN. YOU WERE ARGUING FOR THE SAKE OF ARGUING, WEREN'T YOU? SO THERE ISN'T A DIFFERENCE. I KNOW YOU FEELING THIS CHICK, 'CAUSE YOU WOULDN'T BE IN HERE TRIPPIN IF YOU DIDN'T. THE KEY OF THIS WHOLE

THING WHEN YOU DO APOLOGIZE, IS THAT EVEN IF YOU DON'T MEAN IT NOW, MAKE HER FEEL LIKE YOU DO."

"SO, LIE TO HER IS WHAT YOU'RE TELLING ME?"

"YES AND NO. YOU MIGHT BE LYING NOW, BUT YOU'LL THANK ME LATER, WHEN YOU DO MEAN YOUR APOLOGY."

"AND WHAT I'M POLOGIZING FOR?" HE ASKS.

"NOT LISTENING TO HER AND TAKING HER FEELINGS INTO CONSIDERATION."

"WHAT 'CHU TALKING BOUT? I LISTEN TO HER WHEN I BE GIVING HER THIS PIPE AND SHE BE DAMN HAPPY TOO," HE PROFESSES PROUDLY.

"SO WHY DID SHE NEED A BREAK FROM YOU THEN?! I ASK AS I GAZE AT MY FULL-LENGTH MIRROR ON THE BACK OF MY BEDROOM DOOR. "BOY, JUST DO WHAT I TOLD YOU."

"WHAT IF IT DON'T WORK?"

MORE

"SALEEM, I'M A GIRL, SO I KNOW WHERE SHE'S COMING FROM. NOW COME ON, I GOTTA GET TO THE DENTIST. MY TOOTH IS KILLING ME." I STAND BY THE DOOR, WAITING FOR HIM TO GET OUT OF MY ROOM.

"OH, SHIT. YOU GOING OUT THERE LOOKING LIKE THAT?" HE ASKS TAKING IN THE FULL EFFECT OF MY JEANS, MY "MEAN MUG" T-SHIRT AND FLIP FLOPS.

"YEAH, WHY WHAT'S WRONG WITH MY OUTFIT?" I RESPOND SELF-CONSCIOUSLY LOOKING OVER IT.

HE ASKS, "YOU KNOW ITS POURING BUCKETS OUT THERE, RIGHT?"

I RUN TO THE WINDOW AND PEEK THROUGH THE BLINDS. "SERIOUSLY? AND YOU COULDN'T HAVE TOLD ME THIS BEFORE I GOTTEN DRESSED?"

"MY BAD. YOU KNOW I BE TRIPPIN'" AND WITH THAT HE PULLS OUT HIS CELL. I SNATCH IT OUT HIS HANDS, TO WHICH HE QUESTIONS, "YO, WHAT'S THE DEAL?"

"YOU'RE, TAKING ME TO THE DENTIST."

"BUT I GOTTA CALL TOYA," HE PROTESTS.

AS I WALK THROUGH THE DOORWAY OF MY BEDROOM, I CALL OVER MY SHOULDER AS I SHAKE HIS PHONE IN MY HAND, "YOU CAN DO IT ON OUR WAY." I STOP ONCE I GET TO THE TOP OF THE STAIRS, "OR YOU CAN DO IT WHILE WE WAIT."

DURING THE DRIVE OVER, I COACHED SALEEM ON WHAT EXACTLY TO SAY. GOOD THING HIS GIRL WAS WILLING TO TALK TO HIM FACE-TO-FACE 'CAUSE THE DAY JUST STARTED AND I'M BURNT FROM DEALING WITH THEIR PROBLEMS AND HAVEN'T EVEN BEGUN TO WORK ON MY OWN.

I JUST SAT DOWN AFTER TURNING IN MY LITTLE QUESTIONNAIRE THEY GAVE WHEN I ARRIVED AND IN BURST TWO GUYS LAUGHING WHOLEHEARTEDLY, BOTH NEARLY THE SAME HEIGHT AND BUILD. AROUND 5'9, 185 POUNDS. THE LIGHT BROWN SKIN GUY HAS CURL HAIR, A

MORE

NICE, GROOMED SHADOW OF A BEARD, AND CLEAR SMOOTH SKIN. THE DARKER ONE HAS A HEAD OF WAVES THAT RIVALS THAT OF THE OCEAN AND A THICK BEARD NEATLY CROPPED, FILLED WITH TATTOOS ON HIS FACE, NECK, AND FOREARMS. THEY MUST BE MUSLIMS BECAUSE THEY BOTH HAVE PROMINENT PROSTRATION MARKS ON THE CENTER OF THEIR FOREHEADS. THEIR PANTS, EVEN THOUGH SAGGING, ARE ROLLED UP ABOVE THE ANKLE. DAMN, THEY LOOK GOOD.

I WAS NOTICED BY THEM AS WELL. WHILE LIGHT-BRIGHT APPROACHED

THE DESK, HIS COUNTERPART TOOK A SEAT, LICKING HIS LIPS IN MY DIRECTION. I RUN A HAND THROUGH MY HAIR IN RESPONSE, CROSSED MY LEGS TRYING TO EASE THE TINGLING SENSATION BETWEEN THEM, AND PICKED UP A MAGAZINE.

AS I FLIP THROUGH THE PERIODICAL, I COULD NOT RESIST GLIMPSING IN THEIR DIRECTION. BEAUTIFUL, THEY BOTH ARE AND AS IT HAPPENS, THEY WERE TALKING AND

LOOKING IN MY DIRECTION. WITH A SMILE ON MY FACE, I

CONTINUE TO FLIP THROUGH THE MAGAZINE. I KNOW

THEY FEELING ME, BUT THE CRAZY THING IS THAT I AM

FEELING THE BOTH OF THEM. I HEARD OF THE SAYING

BEFORE, OF HOW "BIRDS OF A FEATHER, FLOCK

TOGETHER," BUT NEVER HAVE I ENCOUNTERED TWO

EQUALLY GOOD-LOOKING DUDES. USUALLY, IT'LL BE

THAT ONE IS FAR BETTER LOOKING THAN THE AVERAGE

ONE.

"MR. ROBINSON?" CALLS THE RECEPTIONIST, AND

THE LIGHT-SKINNED GUY APPROACHES THE DESK. "HERE,

I NEED YOU TO FILL IN A SECTION YOU LEFT BLANK,

PLEASE." HE DOES AND THE RECEPTIONIST THANKS HIM.

HE CALLS OVER HIS SHOULDER, GOING BACK TO

HIS SEAT WITH HIS

EYES FIXATED ON ME, "YOU'RE MORE THAN WELCOME,"

IN THE SEXIEST

DEEP VOICE I HAVE EVER HEARD.

MORE

WHY, OH WHY, DID HE HAVE TO DO THAT? THE TONE OF HIS VOICE EXUDES CONFIDENCE, HIS STRIDE AS WELL. I UNCROSS AND RE-CROSS MY LEGS PRAYING HE CAN'T HEAR MY YEARNING TO BE SCRATCHED RIGHT NOW. TEN MINUTES GOES BY AS WE ALL SHARE STOLEN GLANCES AND I WONDER WHAT'S TAKING THE DENTIST SO LONG.

NOT BEING ABLE TO TAKE IT ANY LONGER, I STAND, WHICH CAPTURED BOTH OF THEIR ATTENTION. I NOD MY HEAD TO THE LEFT AND HEAD THAT WAY, TO THE BATHROOMS. DOWN THE HALL, I TURN THE CORNER AND WAIT DIRECTLY IN FRONT OF THE BATHROOM TO SEE WHICH ONE, IF NOT BOTH, FOLLOWED. THE TENSION BUILDS IN MY CHEST DRAMATICALLY AS THE BEATING OF A DRUM AS I WAIT, HOPING BEYOND HOPE THAT I HADN'T JUST MADE A FOOL OF MYSELF. IT WASN'T UNTIL I HEARD FOOTSTEPS APPROACHING, THAT I WONDERED WHAT I JUST GOT MYSELF INTO. OH WELL, I GUESS IT'S

TOO LATE NOW. AT THE SIGHT OF A FRESH PAIR OF TIMS, I LOOK UP TO SEE WHO CAME.

"MR. ROBINSON," I SAY SEDUCTIVELY.

"SO, YOU WERE PAYING ATTENTION AND SOUNDS LIKE YOU KNOW WHAT YOU WANT," HE REMARKS, CLOSELY EXAMINING MY BODY WITH HIS EYES.

"I ALWAYS DO."

"WHICH IS...?" HE ASKS.

GEES, HIS PROPER SPEECH AND ANNUNCIATION NEARLY MAKES ME PEAK. YET, I SIMPLY REACH OUT AND GRAB THE CROTCH OF HIS PANTS. HIS PENIS IS ERECT AND COULD NOT BE HELD BY ONE HAND ALONE.

"ANYTHING THAT PLEASES ME," I RESPOND.

HE STEPS CLOSER, GENTLY PRESSING MY BACK AGAINST THE WALL. "SO YOU'RE PLEASED?" HE ASKS. "WITH ME."

"YES, MR. ROBINSON."

MORE

"UM, I DON'T THINK I EVER HEARD MY NAME SPOKE LIKE THAT BEFORE. I ENJOY IT," HE ADMITS.

I DIVULGE DEEPER BY ADDING, "DO YOU, MR. ROBINSON?"

"VERY MUCH SO," AND AS HE SAYS THIS, HIS BREATHING QUICKENS.

"SO ARE YOU WILLING TO ACCEPT EVERYTHING? ALL OF MR. ROBINSON?"

"YES. MR. ROBINSON."

WITH THAT, HE EXPOSES HIS ERECTION, 9 INCHES IN LENGTH, 3 IN CIRCUMFERENCE, WHICH IS SLIGHTLY DARKER THAN THE REST OF HIS SKIN TONE. AS HE HOLDS IT IN HIS HAND, HE BEGINS SLOWLY STROKING IT, MOVING THE FORESKIN BACK AND FORTH AS THE HEAD PLAYS PEEK-A-BOO WITH HIS UNCIRCUMGISION.

"WELL?" HE BAITS, AND I JOIN HIM IN LOWERING MY PANTS AND PANTIES.

MORE

THE PRE-CUM FROM HIS PENIS BEGINS TO FLOW AND HE TAKES SOME ONTO HIS FINGERS AND BEGINS TO LUBRICATE MY ANAL HOLE FROM BETWEEN MY LEGS. I LEAN IN TO TASTE HIS SUCCULENT PINK LIPS AND COMBINED WITH HIS THICK TONGUE, THEY DO NOT DISAPPOINT. HE BREAKS AWAY SUDDENLY AND I'M READY TO PROTEST WHEN HE QUICKLY TURNS ME AROUND. FACING THE WALL, HE ENTERS ME FROM BEHIND.

A SILENT MOAN IS ALL THAT COULD ESCAPE MY PARTED LIPS. ALL FROM THE SHEER SIZE OF HIS PENIS, THE SLIGHT PAIN AND PLEASURE THAT HE IS GIVING ME. I LAY MY PALMS FLAT AGAINST THE WALL AND SPREAD MY LEGS AS HE GRABS A HOLD OF MY WAIST AND SLOWLY BACKS IT TOWARDS HIM AS HE WATCHES MY ASS SLIDE FURTHER AND FURTHER ON HIS DICK. HE BEGINS HIS SLOW AND STEADY RHYTHM BY SLIDING ALL THE WAY IN AND ONLY PULLING OUT TO THE SENSITIVE PART OF THE HEAD.

MORE

"ARE YOU ENJOYING YOURSELF?" HE ASKS, VOICE STILL THE SAME CALM AND CONFIDENT, EVEN THOUGH HIS BREATHING IS QUICKER THAN NORMAL.

"YES, MR. ROBINSON."

"AM I PLEASING YOU THE WAY YOU WISH?"

"YES."

"HOW ABOUT NOW?" HE REMOVES HIS RIGHT HAND FROM MY WAIST, FINDS MY CLITORIS AND BEGINS RUBBING IT BETWEEN HIS FINGERS.

"OHH-MY-GOD!"

"SO WOULD I BE CORRECT IF I TAKE THAT TO MEAN A YES?"

"YEA! YES! GOD YES!" PREVIOUSLY, I TRIED TO BE MINDFUL OF THE LEVEL OF MY VOICE, BUT THAT JUST WENT OUT OF THE WINDOW.

"SO, WHAT'S YOUR NAME?"

MORE

DID HE JUST SERIOUSLY ASK ME THAT? I THOUGHT, HERE WE ARE, IN THE HALLWAY OF A DENTIST OFFICE, A PUBLIC SPOT NONETHELESS, GETTING IT IN. ONE OF THE MOST DARING, CRAZY, EXCITING SEXUAL EXPERIENCES I HAVE EVER HAD AND HE WANTS TO KNOW MY NAME. NOW? NEVER MIND HOLDING A CONVERSATION.

"ALI-ANI," I PANT. "CALL...ME...YANI."

"ALIANI, YANI. YOU DON'T LIKE YOUR FULL NAME?"

"I...PREFER...YANI."

"ARE YOU THERE?" HE ASKS.

"WHERE?"

"THERE." AND HE SLIDES HIS FINGERS DEEPER INSIDE MY VAGINA SIMULTANEOUS WITH HIS DICK IN MY ASS AND I RELEASE JUICE UPON JUICES. GOOD," HE SAYS AND WITHIN A FEW MORE STROKES, HE CUMS AS WELL.

WE STAND STILL FOR A MOMENT, TRYING TO CATCH OUR BREATH. I BREAK THE SILENCE BY ASKING, "HOW DID YOU KNOW?"

"SOMETHINGS, I DO."

"AND BY MY MEANING?"

HE PULLS OUT, I TURN AROUND AND FOLLOW HIM INTO THE SINGLE STALL MENS' ROOM. "DID YOU 'MEAN' ANYTHING ELSE?"

WELL, I GUESS HE HAS A POINT THERE. HE GRABS A FEW PAPER TOWELS, WETS THEM AND FIRST CLEANS ME, THEN HIMSELF. AT A KNOCK ON THE DOOR, I JUMP.

"YES?" MR. ROBINSON ANSWERS.

"YO CHRIS MAN, DENTIST BULL LOOKING FOR THAT CHICK MAN, IS SHE IN THERE WIT' YOU?"

"I'LL BE OUT SHORTLY." WAS ALL HE GAVE IN RESPONSE.

MORE

"YEAH, AIGHT." AND I HEAR FOOTSTEPS RETREATING.

"YOUR FRIEND?" I ASK.

"YES. SO, WHAT ARE YOU HAVING DONE TODAY?"

DAMN, I DONE FORGOT ABOUT MY TOOTHACHE. "I HAD A MASSIVE TOOTHACHE THIS MORNING WHICH MADE ME CALL OUT FROM WORK. SUDDENLY, I JUST REMEMBERED, MUST HAVE GOTTEN THE MEDICATION I NEEDED," I SAY WITH A SMILE. "AND YOU" I ASK.

"ROUTINE CHECK-UP AND WHITENING." HE PULLS OUT HIS CELL AND RAISES AN EYEBROW.

I GIVE HIM MY NUMBER AND HE PRESSES THE "CALL" BUTTON. MY PHONE BEGINS VIBRATING IN MY BACK POCKET FURTHERING MY SENSATIONS FROM OUR ORDEAL.

MORE

I END THE CALL. "CHRIS ROBINSON?" I CHECK BEFORE PROGRAMMING IT, WITH THE NUMBER, INTO MY CONTACT LIST.

"YES, AND SPELL ALIANI FOR ME."

"YANI. PLEASE CALL ME YANI."

"YES, OF COURSE," HE ASSURES ME. "BUT I WOULD STILL LIKE TO KNOW, IF YOU DON'T MIND."

"A-L-I-A-N-I"

"ALIANI-?"

"HARRIS. H-A-R-R-I-S."

"AND YANI? Y-A-N-I?"

"EXACTLY."

"CAN I OFFER YOU A RIDE, AFTERWARDS?" AND HE GESTURES TO THE DOOR WITH HIS HAND.

"NO, THAT'S OKAY," I RESPOND WITH A SMILE. I PRESS AND HOLD THE NUMBER 3 ON MY PHONE. "MY

BROTHERS COMING TO PICK ME UP. THANK YOU ANYWAY. DON'T BE A STRANGER." AND I WALK OUT OF THE MENS' ROOM.

CHAPTER 2

I ALREADY KNOCKED TWICE AND STILL HAVEN'T RECEIVED AN ANSWER. I DO NOT FEEL LIKE THIS, THIS MORNING. I'M ALREADY FIFTEEN MINUTES LATE, WITH A POUNDING HEADACHE FROM MY HANGOVER. I KNEW I SHOULDN'T HAVE HAD THAT LAST SHOT LAST NIGHT. LISTENING TO KENDEL'S CRAZY ASS. I KNOW IT WAS HER BIRTHDAY AND ALL, BUT WHAT KIND OF FRIEND WOULD I BE IF I HADN'T TAKEN IT WITH HER?

I KNOCK AGAIN. "MS. JONES, PLEASE OPEN THE DOOR."

"GO AWAY," CAME THE RESPONSE. "I'M NOT EXPECTING ANY VISITORS."
"IT'S ME, MS. HARRIS. YOUR HOME HEALTH CARE AID."

I WAS RELUCTANT TO REPEAT MYSELF, SHE TOOK SO LONG TO UNDO THE LOCKS AND PEER THROUGH THE BARELY CRACKED DOOR TO CHECK MY AUTHENTICITY. HAVING DONE SO, SHE FINALLY GRANTS ME ENTRY TO HER APARTMENT. MUCH TO MY DISMAY, IT IS, AS IT ALWAYS HAS BEEN. THINGS EVERYWHERE. NO MATTER HOW MANY TIMES I TRY TO CLEAN UP AND HELP HER ORGANIZE HER POSSESSIONS, OLD HABITS DIE HARD.

"AND YOU'RE NOT A MISS," SHE INFORMS ME AS SHE SLAMS AND LOCKS THE DOOR BEHIND ME. "WHAT YOU ARE, IS AN UNRELIABLE SELFISH INCONSIDERATE."

"EXCUSE ME?" I RETORT, LYING MY PURSE ON THE COFFEE TABLE AND PROCEED TO THE KITCHEN TO RETRIEVE THE CLEANSERS UNDER THE SINK.

"AND DEAF, SINCE YOU CAN'T A WORD THAT I'M SAYING."

I BEGIN TO FILL A BUCKET WITH SOME HOT WATER. "OH, I HEARD YOU, I JUST WANTED TO KNOW WHAT MADE YOU SAY SOMETHING LIKE THAT."

"CALLING OFF SICK YESTERDAY, COMING UP IN HERE ALL LATE. PROBABLY OUT PARTYING WITH YOUR HOT-IN-THE-PANTS, FAST SELF. I WAS GETTING READY TO CALL THE COMPANY AND REPORT YOU."

I BEGIN IN THE BATHROOM WITH MY CLEANSING BUCKET AND SUPPLIES AND CALL OUT, "WHY DIDN'T YOU?" I KNEW IT WAS A LOW BLOW AND THAT I WOULDN'T RECEIVE RESPONSE.

MS. JONES HAD QUITE A FEW AIDES BEFORE ME SINCE SHE CAME TO LIVE IN THIS GATED SENIOR CENTER. IT DIDN'T TAKE ME PAST THE FIRST TWO OR THREE DAYS TO FIGURE OUT WHY. SHE'S A TOUGH, NO NONSENSE COOKIE, AND SET IN HER WAYS. AND GRANTED, THIS IS

HOW OUR RELATIONSHIP HAS BEEN FOR THE PAST THREE MONTHS, I'M THE LONGEST STANDING AIDE THAT SHE HAS HAD.

FINISHED WITH THE BATHROOM, I SET THE CLEANING SUPPLIES ASIDE AND MOVE ON TO THE DISHES. I HEAR, FROM THE FLOOR MODEL T.V. THAT SHE'S WATCHING ONE OF HER PROGRAMS. I KNOW SHE DOESN'T LIKE TO BE DISTURBED AND MISS ANYTHING, SO I WAIT TILL IT GOES TO COMMERCIAL TO ASK, "HOW WAS YOUR DAY YESTERDAY?"

"HUMPH, DISAPPOINTING."

FIGURES. "HOW SO?" I ASK SINCE I NEVER SAW HER SMILE OR HEAR HER LAUGH. SHOOT, EVEN SPEAK GOOD OF ANYBODY FOR THAT MATTER.

"WELL, FOR ONE, I WAS HUNGRY."

THAT STOPPED ME IN MY TRACK. I TURN AROUND TO FACE HER. "WHO FILLED IN FOR ME YESTERDAY?"

"SOME CHILD, SWORE SHE KNEW EVERYTHING TOO. COULDN'T TELL HER NOTHING," SHE ANSWERED BITTERLY.

"SHE DIDN'T FEED YOU?"

"I DON'T KNOW THAT CHILD. I WASN'T PUTTING ANYTHING IN ME SHE TOUCHED. WHEN SHE LEFT, I OPENED A CAN OF EM PORK-N-BEANS AND ATE 'EM."

"O.K." I RINSE AND DRY MY HANDS. "WHAT DO YOU WANT TO EAT?"

"NO, GO AHEAD AND FINISH CLEANING," SHE PROTESTS.

"THE CLEANING CAN WAIT. NOW, TELL ME WHAT YOU WANT." STUBBORN OLD LADY, IS WHAT I WANTED TO ADD.

SHE THINKS FOR A MOMENT, THEN AT THE SOUND OF HER PROGRAMS THEME MUSIC, SHE SAYS, "I DON'T CARE, FOOD. NOW, BE QUIET."

RIGHT, AND IF I HADN'T OFFERED TO COOK FOR YOU, SURELY YOU WOULD HAVE REPORTED *THAT* TO HOME BASE.

I GENTLY OPEN THE DOOR OF THE NEXT APARTMENT. "MISS ZUICK?" I CALL OUT.

SHE STICKS HER HEAD OUT OF THE BATHROOM DOOR. "YES DEAR,
COME ON IN."

I CLOSE THE DOOR AFTER I DO. "MM, IT SMELLS GOOD IN HERE, FRUITY."

"HAVE A SEAT; I'LL BE OUT IN A MOMENT."

I NOTICE THAT SHE HAS THREE DIFFERENT MAGAZINES LAID OUT ON THE COFFEE TABLE. WHEN I TAKE A SEAT, I NOTICE EACH OF THEM, KNITTING/QUILTING PATTERNS, HOME DECOR, AND LOGIC PUZZLES. MY ATTENTION GETS GRABBED JUST AS I WAS GOING TO REACH FOR ONE AS MISS ZUICK COMES

OUT CARRYING A PAIL IN ONE AND A SPONGE IN THE OTHER.

"WHEW," SHE WIPES THE PERSPIRATION OFF THE TOP OF HER FOREHEAD WITH THE BACK OF HER SPONGE FILLED HAND. "SO, HOW ARE YOU DOING THIS FINE DAY? I HEARD YOU WERE SICK YESTERDAY."

"MISS ZUICK, WERE YOU REALLY JUST IN THERE CLEANING THE BATHROOM?"

"OH CHILD, A LITTLE EXERCISE ISN'T GONNA HURT AN OLD BITTY LIKE ME."

"AND THAT PIE IN THE OVEN?" I ASK INCREDULOUSLY. SHE PUTS THE CLEANING SUPPLIES AWAY. "WHAT CAN I SAY YANI? GUILTY AS CHARGED." AND SHE SHRUGS HER SHOULDERS.

"YOU DO KNOW THAT IT IS MY JOB TO DO THESE THINGS FOR YOU, DON'T YOU?" I REMIND HER.

"SURE, I DO. BUT YOU MOST CERTAINLY AREN'T GOING TO TAKE AWAY FROM ME THE THINGS I ENJOY MOST, ARE YOU?" SHE ASKS, LOOKING ALL PITIFUL, TRYING TO MAKE ME FEEL GUILTY.

"OF COURSE NOT. WHY DID YOU SIGN UP FOR AN AIDE, IF YOU DO EVERYTHING FOR YOURSELF?" WAS MY SINCERE QUESTION.

"WHY, FOR THE COMPANY; COMPANIONSHIP. I BEEN YEARNING FOR IT FOR SO LONG AFTER MY DAUGHTER AMIEE WENT AGAINST MY ADVICE AND JOINED THAT CULT WHERE THAT FRAUD, KNOWINGLY, POISONED THAT KOOL-AID. I SHUT MYSELF IN AFTERWARDS, CUTTING MYSELF OFF FROM ALL OF SOCIETY. BESIDES THE T.V., UP UNTIL RECENTLY, HAVE I STARTED TO REALLY MEET PEOPLE."

"BUT HOW? YOU STILL DON'T LEAVE THE BUILDING."

MORE

SHE TAKES THE PIE OUT OF THE OVEN AND PLACES IT ON THE STOVE TOP. "VERY TRUE. VERY TRUE, INDEED. HOWEVER, THERE'S THE YOUNG MAN, JEREMY, WHO DELIVERS MY GROCERIES. IN THE EVENINGS I JOIN SOME OF THE OTHER LADIES IN THE LOUNGE TO CHAT AND THE GOSSIP THEY EXCHANGE, OH I GET MY FILL." SHE FINDS HER WAY TO THE SEAT NEXT TO ME AND SAYS, "AND THEN, THERE'S ALWAYS YOU DARLING."

"YEAH, BUT THERE'S A WHOLE BIG WORLD BEYOND THIS BUILDING'S WALLS. DON'T YOU FEEL AS THOUGH YOU'RE MISSING OUT?" I ASK.

"SWEETY, THERE'S NOTHING OUT THERE FOR ME. AND WHO'S TO SAY I CAN'T BE HAPPY COOPED UP, RIGHT HERE? HUNH? NOW, THAT'S ENOUGH ABOUT MY SILLY OLD SELF. WHAT'S GOING ON WITH YOU? YOU SEEM TO BE IN A CHEERFULLY, CHATTY MOOD CONSIDERING WHERE YOU JUST CAME FROM."

"WELL, YOU KNOW MS. JONES. SHE IS WHO SHE IS." I SIGH.

"I BELIEVE SHE TREATS PEOPLE THAT WAY BECAUSE NONE OF HER CHILDREN EVER COMES TO VISIT," MISS ZUICK THEORIZES.

"SHE HAS CHILDREN?!" SHOCKED, I ASK.

"MM-HMM. 4."

"WOW, AND TO THINK HOW BADLY SHE MUST HAVE TREATED THEM, FOR THEM NOT TO COME AND VISIT HER."

"WELL, AS I HEAR IT, AND YOU DIDN'T HEAR THIS FROM ME, BUT SHE SUPPOSEDLY SPOILED THEM ROTTEN AND WHEN HER HUSBAND PAST, THE CHILDREN SPLIT THE INSURANCE MONEY, SHIPPED HER HERE AND NEVER LOOKED BACK."

"I GUESS SHE SMOTHERED THEM SO MUCH, THAT THEY JUST RAN AS FAST AS THEY COULD, THE FIRST CHANCE THAT THEY GOT."

"YOU SAID IT, NOT ME." AND I JOIN HER IN A CHUCKLE. SHE THEN ASKS, "ARE YOU NOT EVEN GOING TO TELL ME HIS NAME?"

I WAS SO THROWN OFF BY HER DIRECTNESS THAT I HAD TO ASK HER TO REPEAT HERSELF. I KNOW WE'VE BEEN IN A CONSTANT CONVERSATION SINCE I CAME IN, BUT TRUTH BE KNOWN, I WAS THINKING ABOUT HIM.

"OH, NOBODY. JUST SOMEONE I MET AT THE DENTIST OFFICE YESTERDAY. JUST BEFORE I HAD MY WISDOM TOOTH PULLED; NOTHING MAJOR."

"HE SIMPLY CANNOT BE A NOBODY, OR NOTHING MAJOR IF YOU 'RE GLOWING LIKE YOU ARE. THIS IS THE FIRST TIME I HAVEN'T HEARD YOU COMPLAIN AFTER COMING FROM MS. JONES' PLACE."

SHE HAS A POINT ON THAT ONE. "HIS NAME'S CHRIS."

"WAIT, WAIT. EXCUSE ME FOR INTERRUPTING. I KNOW THAT I AM GOING TO ENJOY THIS, BUT LET'S TAKE THIS ONE STEP FURTHER, SHALL WE?" AND SHE STANDS AND HEADS FOR THE KITCHEN. SHE OPENS THE FREEZER AND PULLS SOMETHING OUT. TURNING AROUND, SHE ASKS, "APPLE PIE A LA MODE ANYONE? FRENCH VANILLA, OF COURSE." BEFORE I HAD A CHANCE TO PROTEST, SHE PULLS TWO BOWLS FROM THE DISH RACK AND BEGINS TO FILL THEM.

"MS. ZUICK, HONESTLY, THERE ISN'T *TOO* MUCH TO TELL." OR THAT I AM GOING TO TELL.

"OH, DON'T BE SO MODEST HONEY. THERE MUST BE SOMETHING ABOUT HIM THAT'S GOT YOU INTERESTED."

TELL ME ABOUT IT, I THINK TO MYSELF. "HE'S CUTE, WELL SPOKEN AND WE EXCHANGED NUMBERS. END OF STORY."

MORE

SHE COMES BACK OVER AND RECLAIMS HER SEAT, PASSING ME A SPOON AND BOWL. "NOW, I RECALL A YOUNG LADY TELLING ME, THERE'S MORE TO LIFE BEYOND THESE WALLS. SO INDULGE ME. I COULD ONLY HOPE I DID NOT MAKE THIS PIE FOR NOTHING."

DID SHE JUST TRY TO HIT ME WITH THE GUILT TRIP? AND DAMN IT DID I KNOWINGLY FALL FOR IT. I BEGIN TO GIVE HER A DESCRIPTION OF CHRIS, LEAVING A BIG PART OUT, I MIGHT ADD. AS SOON AS I PLOP THE FIRST SPOONFUL OF MY WARM/COOL TREAT INTO MY MOUTH, MY CELL BEGINS TO RING.

I CHEW AND SWALLOW AS FAST AS I COULD, WITHOUT CHOKING, AND ANSWER MY PHONE. "EXCUSE ME," I SAY TO MISS ZUICK, THEN INTO THE PHONE, "HELLO?"

"YES, MAY I SPEAK TO YANI?" GOES THE DEEP, CONFIDENT VOICE.

MORE

I CHECK THE CALLER I.D. AND POINT TO THE PHONE, SILENTLY MOUTHING TO MISS ZUICK THAT IT'S HIM. "THIS ME CHRIS. I'M GLAD YOU REMEMBERED, BUT I'M WITH A CLIENT RIGHT NOW." MISS ZUICK TAPS ME AND SHAKES HER HEAD NO. SHE MIMICS TALKING WITH HER HANDS.

"I DO APOLOGIZE. I DIDN'T REALIZE YOU WERE AT WORK. IS THERE A TIME WHEN I COULD CALL YOU BACK? OR WOULD YOU RATHER CALL ME WHEN YOU BECOME AVAILABLE?" HE ASKS.

MISS ZUICK WHISPERS IN MY EAR TO PLACE THE CALL ON SPEAKERPHONE AND FOLLOWS HER REQUEST WITH A SAD PUPPY DOG FACE. UNABLE TO DENY, I DO, WHICH INSTANTLY BRIGHTENS HER FACE WITH A SMILE.

"ACTUALLY, SHE'S ALLOWING ME TO TAKE THE CALL. WHAT'S UP?"

"DO YOU REALLY HAVE THAT TYPE OF EFFECT ON EVERYONE YOU MEET?" HE ASKS SEDUCTIVELY, WHICH PROMPTED AN INQUISITIVE LOOK FROM MISS ZUICK.

"ONLY A SELECT FEW," WAS ALL MY COYNESS WOULD ALLOW ME TO RESPOND.

"SO WHAT TYPE OF WORK DO YOU DO?"

"I TAKE CARE OF PEOPLE."

"I'D SAY SO," CHRIS RESPONDS AND MISS ZUICK GIGGLES, INTERRUPTING HIM. I DOUBT HE NOTICED THE SLIGHT DISTINCTION BETWEEN HER AND MY LAUGHTER, AS HE CONTINUED. "SO, WOULD IT BOTHER YOU IF I PICKED YOU UP AFTER YOU GET OFF?"

"NO, THAT'LL BE COOL."

"AND WHAT TIME WILL YOU BE GETTING OFF EXACTLY?"

THANKS TO MISS ZUICK PROVIDING A QUICK RESPONSE, I RELAYED, "30 MINUTES." I, THEN, GAVE HIM

MORE

THE ADDRESS TO THE GATED SENIOR APARTMENT BUILDING AND TOLD HIM TO LET ME KNOW WHEN HE GOT HERE.

"MY-MY, CHARMING YOUNG MAN, ISN'T HE? THERE'S NO WONDER AS TO WHY YOU'RE ATTRACTED TO HIM. HE SEEMS PRETTY WELL-SPOKEN FOR A GUY YOUR AGE. WAIT, HOW OLD ARE YOU AGAIN?" MISS ZUICK INQUIRES.

"ACTUALLY, I DON'T HOW OLD HE IS. I'M 22."

"WELL, LET'S ENJOY SOME MORE OF THIS PIE BEFORE YOU GET GOING. AND BEFORE YOU COME IN TOMORROW, I WOULD LIKE YOU TO DO A FAVOR FOR ME."

"OK, WHAT IS IT? YOU KNOW I DON'T HAVE A PROBLEM GETTING THINGS FOR YOU," I ASSURE HER.

HER SMILE WAS NOT ONE SIMPLY OF HAPPINESS BUT MISCHIEVOUS. "TAKE A PICTURE OF HIM SO THAT I CAN SEE WHAT HE LOOKS LIKE."

MORE

CHAPTER 3

I MEET AND GREET CHRIS IN FRONT OF THE BUILDING, RIGHT WHERE HE STATED THAT HE WOULD BE, LEANING ON A SILVER ACURA.

"DO YOU HAVE ANY PLANS?" HE ASKS.

"MM, NO?"

"YOU HESITATED, ANY REASON AS TO WHY?"

"NO, JUST THAT I GOT OFF FROM WORK A LITTLE EARLIER THAN USUAL AND I KNOW THAT MY PHONE WILL BE RINGING OFF THE HOOK IN ABOUT AN HOUR OR TWO."

"WE HAVE ENOUGH TIME THEN," HE EXPLAINS, OPENING THE PASSENGER SIDE DOOR FOR ME. FOR A QUICK SECOND, I THINK ABOUT STEPPING IN, EYES

DARTING BACK AND FORTH BETWEEN HIM AND THE CAR.

PUSHING ALL DOUBT ASIDE, I CLIMB IN ASKING, "FOR?"

"YOU SHARED YOUR WORK WITH ME, I JUST

WANTED TO RECIPROCATE." AND HE CLOSES MY DOOR.

ONCE WE'VE GOTTEN ON THE ROAD, I ASK, "SO,

WHAT IS IT THAT YOU DO?"

HE BRIEFLY FLASHES THAT BRILLIANT WHITE

SMILE OF HIS. "I PREFER TO ALLOW MY WORK TO SPEAK

FOR ITSELF."

O-KAY. SO, HE IS SO TOTALLY DIFFERENT THAN

ANY TYPE OF GUY I TALKED TO BEFORE. THAT'S A GIVEN.

"HOW OLD ARE YOU?"

"TWENTY-ONE. MAY I ASK THE SAME OF YOU?"

"TWENTY-TWO. YOU CAME TO PICK ME UP PRETTY

QUICK, WHAT, DO YOU LIVE AROUND HERE OR

SOMETHING?" I ASK, THINKING A YOUNG ONE.

INTERESTING.

MORE

I WAS ACTUALLY JUST FINISHING UP WITH A POTENTIAL CLIENT WHEN I CALLED YOU, NOT TO FAR FROM WHERE YOU WERE LOCATED. BUT I ACTUALLY LIVE DOWN 'THE BOTTOM'."

"NO WAY. MY CLOSEST GIRLFRIEND LIVES DOWN THERE AND I BE OVER HER HOUSE ALL THE TIME. WHERE AT?"

"AT 34TH AND MT. VERNON."

"AT 34TH AND MT. VERNON? THERE ISN'T ANY APARTMENT BUILDINGS UP THERE."

"I NEVER SAID I LIVED IN APARTMENTS."

"OH, YOU HAVE A ROOMMATE. WHO DO YOU LIVE WITH?"

THERE'S A MOMENT BEFORE HE RESPONDS. "NO ONE, I OWN MY OWN TWO BEDROOM HOME AND THIS CAR."

THIS IS BETTER THAN I EXPECTED.

MORE

"NEED I PROMPT YOU WITH YOUR OWN QUESTIONS?" HE ASKS.

"I LIVE WITH ONE OF MY BROTHERS, IN MY CHILDHOOD HOME, DOWN 10TH AND DIAMOND, MY FATHER IS HARDLY EVER THERE. IT'S BEEN ME AND MY BROTHERS FENDING FOR OURSELVES THAT IT'S MORE OR LESS OUR HOUSE."

"WHAT'S YOUR FATHERS' OCCUPATION?"

"TRYING NOT TO OVERDOSE, JUST SO THAT HE CAN HAVE ONE MORE CHANCE AT GETTING HIGH."

"OH, I APOLOGIZE," HE REMARKS SOMBERLY.

"NO BIG DEAL. DON'T WORRY ABOUT IT."

" AND YOUR BROTHERS?"

"SALEEM, MY YOUNGER BROTHER WHO I LIVE WITH, HE'S A STICK-UP ARTIST. KUERON SUPPOSED TO BE COMING HOME SOON FROM UPSTATE FOR ARMED ROBBERY AND AGGRAVATED ASSAULT. THAT'S IF HE

HASN'T CAUGHT ANOTHER CHARGE UP THERE LIKE HE

DID THE LAST TIME."

SILENCE ENTERS THE CAR MOMENTARILY AGAIN

AS HE REFLECTS ON WHAT I JUST TOLD HIM. WHEN HE

FINALLY DID SPEAK, HE TELLS ME THAT HE NEVER MET

HIS FATHER, HE WAS HIS MOTHER'S ONLY CHILD AND

UNFORTUNATELY, SHE WAS ONE OF THE CASUALTIES IN 9/11.

SHOOT, HERE I WAS THINKING MY FAMILY SITUATION

WAS BAD. I CAN'T EVEN IMAGINE BEING ALL ALONE IN

THE WORLD. I WANTED TO ASK IF HIS RADIO WORKED, AT

LEAST TO KEEP THE SILENCE AT BAY, BUT I FELT AS

THOUGH, IN SOME WAY, IT WOULD BE DISRESPECTFUL.

BY NOW, AS I VIEW OUT OF THE WINDOW, I NOTICE THAT

WE ARE IN SOUTH PHILADELPHIA.

AFTER FINDING A PARKING SPOT ON 11TH, JUST SHY

OF THE INTERSECTION AT SOUTH STREET, HE ASKS ME AM

I READY. WITHOUT ANY RESERVATIONS, I AM, AND HE

PROCEEDS IN HELPING ME OUT OF THE CAR.

AS WE BEGIN WALKING, HE ASKS, "ARE YOU AN OPEN-MINDED PERSON?"

AS STRANGE AS THE QUESTION SEEMED, THE WAY HE ASKED, MADE IT SEEM LIKE HE GENUINELY WANTED TO KNOW. "I GUESS SO, YEAH."

"DO YOU KNOW WHAT ABSTRACT IS?"

"SOMETHING DIFFERENT, RIGHT?"

"MORE OR LESS. YOU'LL SEE," HE SAYS AND OPENS A BACK DOOR.

"AFTER YOU."

AS MY EYES ADJUST TO THE LIGHTING OF THE ROOM, I TAKE A LOOK AROUND. STRATEGICALLY DECORATED ON THE WALLS, ARE PAINTINGS AMID SCULPTURES SPORADICALLY SPACED OUT. "YOU WORK IN A MUSEUM? OKAY."

YET, HE WAS QUICK TO CORRECT, WITHOUT THE LEAST BIT OF JUDGEMENT. "THIS IS AN ART GALLERY,

MORE

WHERE PEOPLE CAN BUY A PIECE, IF THEY LIKE." AS WE

BEGIN TO MOVE ABOUT THE ROOM, VIEWING THE

PAINTINGS, HE CONTINUES, "I WOULDN'T SAY THAT I

HAVE A CERTAIN TIME TO WHERE I HAVE TO COME IN,

THOUGH,"

"I DON'T UNDERSTAND, HOW DO YOU GET PAID, IF

YOU DON'T COME IN TO WORK?"

"ALL IN DUE TIME YANI, ALL IN DUE TIME."

WE APPROACH ONE PARTICULAR PAINTING WHERE

HE ASKS ME OF MY OPINION. ALBEIT I'M NOT BIG ON

PAINTINGS, BUT LET'S JUST GIVE IT A TRY. WHAT THE

HELL? THE PAINTING IS OF RED, PURPLE, ORANGE AND

BLUE VERTICAL, DIAGONAL AND HORIZONTAL LINES.

THE LINES DIRECT MY EYES DOWNWARD, TO A HEART

WHICH IS TORN OPEN, NEARLY IN HALF, AS IF LIGHTNING

STRUCK IT. THE BOTTOM OF THE PAINTING IS BLACK,

AND GETS LIGHTER GOING TOWARDS THE TOP, YET NOT

QUITE GETTING WHITE.

MORE

"IT'S CERTAINLY NOT HAPPY, THAT'S FOR SURE."

"YES, BUT HOW DOES IT MAKE YOU FEEL?" HE ASKS.

"LET'S SEE, CONFUSED. I'D SAY THE PAINTER WAS DEPRESSED, SAD AND POSSIBLY A LITTLE ANGRY."

"HOW DID YOU KNOW?"

"HOW DID I KNOW WHAT?"

"THAT THEY WERE MY EXACT FEELINGS?"

I LOOK FROM THE PAINTING, BACK TO HIM, OPEN MOUTHED AND HE NODDED HIS HEAD WITH A SMILE. HE POINTED ME IN THE DIRECTION OF A POSTER DISPLAYING "THE OTHER SIDE STUDIOS, FEATURING: CHRISTOPHER ROBINSON."

"WHY DIDN'T YOU TELL ME?" I ASK HIM, STILL TRYING TO PIECE IT ALL TOGETHER IN MY MIND.

"I WANTED TO GET SOME HONEST FEEDBACK. MOST PEOPLE, WHEN THEY KNOW BEFORE HAND I

CREATED A PIECE, THEY TELL ME WHAT THEY THINK I WANT TO HEAR. THIS PARTICULAR PAINTING WAS CREATED AFTER THE LOSS OF MY MOTHER. CONTRARY TO POPULAR BELIEF, IT IS MY BEST SELLER."

"WITH THE WAY THE WORLD IS TODAY, I GUESS THERE'S A LOT OF PEOPLE OUT THERE WHO CAN RELATE TO PAIN."

WE VIEW THE REMAINING WORKS OF ART, MOST OF WHICH, WAS OF HIS OWN. THEN AFTER, WE RETURNED TO HIS CAR. DURING THE DRIVE, WE LEARNED MORE OF EACH OTHER. EXPRESSING LIKES AND DISLIKES, FINDING OUT THAT THERE ISN'T TOO MANY DIFFERENCES BETWEEN US. NEITHER OF US SMOKE YET REMARKED THAT IT WOULDN'T BOTHER US IF THE OTHER DID. WE BOTH ARE INTERESTED IN THE ARTS, HIS BEING OBVIOUSLY, THE ABSTRACT, WHILE MINE'S, THE PERFORMING, MUSIC, DANCE AND THEATRE.

MORE

HE ASKED HAVE I EVER BEEN TO THE THEATRE AND I INFORMED HIM OF MY ONLY EXPERIENCE BEING, WAS IN MY PERFORMING ARTS HIGH SCHOOL, WHERE WE PUT ON SHOWS. I PERFORMED IN A FEW, BUT ONLY IN THE ASPECT OF DANCING. THE CONVERSATION MOVED ON TO FOOD AND I SHARED OF HOW I NEVER VENTURED OUT MY COMFORTS OF SOUL FOOD TO WHICH HG OBLIGED HE WAS HAPPY TO ASSIST ME IN BROADENING MY TASTE PALATES HORIZONS.

CAUGHT UP IN THE CONVERSATION, I DIDN'T REALIZE OUR SURROUNDINGS UNTIL HE ASKED WHICH ONE WAS MINE. I LOOKED OUT OF THE WINDSHIELD AND NOTICED WE WERE DESCENDING DIAMOND STREET, TOWARDS 10TH.

"CROSS THE INTERSECTION, 3RD DOOR FROM THE CORNER," WAS MY RESPONSE, EYES CAST DOWNWARD TOWARD MY CLASPED HANDS. NOT WANTING OUR GOOD TIME TO END.

MORE

CHRIS PARKS AND I SEE SALEEM SITTING OUT FRONT WITH TOYA IN HIS LAP. "YOUR BROTHER, CORRECT?" CHRIS INQUIRES.

I NOD MY ACKNOWLEDGMENT, ONCE AGAIN, EYES DOWNCAST.HOWEVER, THEY WERE NOT THERE FOR LONG AS HE PLACED HIS HAND ATOP MINE. I LOOK INTO HIS EYES.

"I ENJOYED OUR TIME TOGETHER THIS AFTERNOON. YESTERDAY AS WELL."

"I DID, TOO," I RESPOND.

"AND, IF YOU WOULD PERMIT IT, I WOULD APPRECIATE IT IF YOU WOULD ACCOMPANY ME TO A PARTY THIS EVENING."

"PARTY? YEAH, I LOVE PARTIES. WAIT," I HAD TO CHECK MYSELF. "WHAT KIND OF PARTY? IS THERE GOING TO BE SOME KIND OF DRESS CODE OR SOMETHING?"

"THE PARTY IS TO CELEBRATE AND HONOR MY WORK BEING FEATURED IN THE ART GALLERY. TO MY KNOWLEDGE, I DON'T BELIEVE THERE WILL BE A DRESS CODE."

"SO, WHAT TIME WILL YOU BE PICKING ME UP?" I ASK.

"HOW'S 8?"

I CHECK THE TIME ON MY PHONE. THREE HOURS. "YOU CERTAINLY DON'T GIVE A GIRL MUCH TIME TO GET READY, DO YOU?"

"I GUESS I JUST WANTED TO SEE HOW YOU MOVE," HE EMPHASIZES, "UNDER PRESSURE."

CHAPTER 4

WALKING PAST THE TWO LOVE BIRDS, I CRUISE RIGHT IN THE FRONT DOOR ON CLOUD NINE, NOT EVEN PAYING ATTENTION TO WHAT SALEEM WAS SAYING.

"DAG, IT TOOK YOU LONG ENOUGH," KENDLE EXPRESSES IN AN AGGRAVATED TONE. "WHAT TOOK YOU SO LONG? WHAT YOU FORGOT YOU WAS SUPPOSED TO BE HELPING ME DO MY INDIVIDUALS? SHE ASKS BARELY A QUARTER OF THE WAY DONE.

"YEAH, BUT GIRL, WAIT TILL I TELL YOU…,"

"YANI, THAT'S HOW YOU DOIN A BROTHA? JUST GONNA IG ME LIKE THAT?" YELLS SALEEM WALKING THROUGH THE DOOR WITH TOYA FRESH ON HIS HEELS.

"KEN, LET ME TELL YOU HOW…," AGAIN, I GET INTERRUPTED BY SALEEM AS HE GRABS MY HAND.

"SERIOUSLY?!" HE BOOMS.

"ARE *YOU* SERIOUS?" I RETORT, SNATCHING MY ARM AWAY.

MORE

"WHO DA FUCK WAS DAT IN DA CAR?"

"I WAS JUST EXPLAINING IT BEFORE I WAS SO RUDELY INTERRUPTED. WHY? WHAT'S IT TO YOU?" I QUESTION WITH A ROLL OF THE NECK, PLACING MY HAND ON MY HIP.

"I JUST WANTED TO KNOW SO THAT WHEN KUERON COMES HOME ON MONDAY, WANTING TO SEE EVERYBODY, I'LL BE SURE TO TELL HIM THAT INSTEAD OF TRYNA LOOK FOR CHARLES." HE GRIMACES AS HE SAYS THE NAME, "WHOSE BEEN GONE OVER A WEEK BINGING, AFTER STEALING YOUR CHECK, YOU WERE OUT THERE ROLLING AROUND WITH SOME NIGGA I AIN'T EVEN MET."

"MONDAY?" I ASK.

"YEAH," HE ANSWERS, SARCASTICALLY.

"MM- GIRL, I LOVE YOU AND ALL, BUT YOU KNOW KUE DON'T PLAY THAT," COMMENTS KENDLE.

MORE

"LIKE, OH MY GOD, SHUT UP," I RESPOND, SLIGHTLY

FRUSTRATED.

"SO WHAT'S THE PLAN, LEEM-BABY?" TOYA ASKS

OF HIM IN AN ALMOST CHILDLIKE OF A WHINE. THAT JUST

MADE ME MORE ANNOYED AND TEMPTS A HEADACHE

EVEN FURTHER.

HE WRAPS ONE OF HIS LONG LINKY ARMS AROUND

HER WAIST AND KISSES HER ON HER FOREHEAD. "DON'T

KNO', BABY GIRL, THAT'S WHY I WANTED TO TALK TO MS.

BRAINIAC RIGHT HERE," HE SAYS IN A DEEP SEDUCTIVE

VOICE.

I SWEAR IF THE TITLE "DUMB AND DUMBER"

DOESN'T FIT THESE TWO

THEN I'M AT A TOTAL LOST.

"SO, WHAT'LL IT BE, LIL' G?" HE ASKS REFERRING TO

ME BY MY FAMILY GIVEN NICKNAME. ONE I HAVEN'T

BEEN CALLED SINCE KUERON WENT AWAY, SOMEHOW, IT

MADE SINCE BACK THEN. BOTH OF MY BROTHERS, BEING

MORE

NOTORIOUS HOOD STARS, OR GANGSTERS, AS THEIR LITTLE SISTER, "LIL 'G" JUST STUCK. THAT IS UNTIL I MADE THE DECISION TO COME OUT FROM UNDERNEATH OF THEIR SHADOW AND LIVE MY OWN LIFE.

"I GOT IT. IT'S SIMPLE, REALLY. YOU FIND HIM AND I'LL NURSE HIM BACK TO HEALTH." I MOTION TO KENDLE. "COME ON GIRL, I'M ON A TIGHT SCHEDULE."

"HOLD UP, THAT'S YOUR PLAN? SO, YOU GET TO RUN THE STREETS WHILE I SEARCH FOR HIM? HOW IS THAT FAIR?"

HALFWAY UP THE STEPS, I RESPOND, "WOULD YOU LIKE TO BE NURSING A DETOXING ADDICT? CLEANING UP VOMIT AND WHATEVER ELSE?"

"AIGHT, AND YOU CAN GET HIM STRAIGHT BEFORE KUE GETS HOME IN

THREE DAYS?" SALEEM ASKS.

MORE

"NOT IF YOU DON'T GET A MOVE ON IT, *'LEEM BABY'*," I MOCK, IN MY ROOM, I THROW THE DOUBLE CLOSET DOOR OPEN. "TSK, MAN. I KNEW IT. I DON'T HAVE ANYTHING TO WEAR." I JUST DID LAUNDRY TWO DAYS AGO.

KENDLE FINALLY FINISHES BOUNCING ON MY BED AND REMARKS, "FOR

WHAT? WHERE ARE WE GOING?"

"SORRY BOOPS, NOT THIS TIME." CHECKING THE TIME, I CONTINUE WALKING OVER TO HER. "WHAT I WAS TRYING TO TELL YOU EARLIER, WAS THAT THE GUY THAT I MET YESTERDAY IS TAKING ME OUT TONIGHT."

"AND YOU JUST NOW TELLING ME? WHO, CHRIS? WHERE HE FROM? WHAT HE—" SHE WAS SPEAKING SO RAPIDLY, THEN SUDDENLY BROKE OFF. I FOLLOW HER GAZE TO FIND TOYA STANDING AT MY DOOR.

"LEEM TOLD ME TO STAY HERE UNTIL HE GOT BACK," SHE SAYS AS IF SHE HAD NO OTHER CHOICE,

PROUDLY PUTTING WAY TOO MUCH EFFORT INTO THAT PIECE OF CHEWING GUM.

KENDLE LOOKS AT ME WITH DISGUST. YOU SEE, THE THING IS, TOYA GREW UP RIGHT AROUND THE CORNER IN THE NORRIS STREET PROJECTS HIGH RISE. SHE AND I GREW UP TOGETHER, GOING TO SCHOOL TOGETHER UP TO THE EIGHTH GRADE. I MET KENDLE IN HIGH SCHOOL AND IT WAS SHE WHO FIRST POINTED OUT TO ME THAT OF HOW TOYA HAS NO DRIVE NOR DREAMS IN LIFE, NOTHING TO STRIVE FOR, ONLY BEING CONTENT WITH GOVERNMENT HANDOUTS. SHOOT, ANY HANDOUTS FOR THAT MATTER. PROBABLY HAND-ME-DOWNS AS WELL. SO UNLIKE KENDLE AND MYSELF, BUT WHAT THE HELL, I COULD USE THE HELP RIGHT NOW.

I BEGIN ON THE RIGHT SIDE OF KENDLE'S HEAD, OPPOSITE OF WHAT SHE HAD ALREADY STARTED. "OKAY, HEY IF YOU DON'T MIND, COULD YOU HELP ME FIGURE OUT WHAT IN THE WORLD I AM GOING TO WEAR TO THIS PARTY TONIGHT? I HAVE TO HELP THIS CHILD DO THIS

MORE

HAIR." I ASK OF TOYA FOCUSING MY ATTENTION BACK ON KENDLE, "UNH-UNH GIRL, DON'T STOP JUST 'CAUSE I STARTED. WE ON BORROWED TIME AS IT IS."

"COME ON, NOW YANI, YOU KNOW YOU BRAID FASTER THAN I DO." SHE POUTS.

"BUT STILL, THE QUICKER WE CAN GET FINISHED, THE BETTER." CHECKING OUT MY WARDROBE, TOYA ASKS, "WHAT TYPE OF PARTY IS IT?"

"YEAH, YOU AIN'T FINISHED TELLING ME ABOUT MR. HUNG LOW," ADDS KENDLE.

I LAUGH, "GIRL, YOU CRAZY. I CAN COUNT ON YOU TO REMEMBER THAT PART, NOW CAN'T I?"

"YOU KNOW ME, HE AIN'T GOOD UNLESS HE GOT THE GOODS," KENDLE PROUDLY PROFESSES.

"ALL HE TOLD ME WAS THAT THE PARTY WAS TO CELEBRATE HIS NEW JOB."

"AND THAT IS?" KENDLE ASKS.

MORE

HMM? HOW DO I EXPLAIN THIS SO THAT THE BOTH OF THEM CAN UNDERSTAND WITHOUT ME HAVING TO CLARIFY, OR WITHOUT CRITICISM.

"HE DOES MURALS."

KENDLE WAS THE FIRST TO RESPOND, AS I EXPECTED SINCE SHE'S ABLE TO RELATE IN THE ASPECT OF HER POETRY AND CREATIVE WRITING.

"OH YEAH, AN ARTIST, HUNH? YOU SEE ANY OF HIS WORK?"

"YEAH, AND HE'S GOOD TOO."

"HEELS OR SNEAKERS?" TOYA ASKS.

I LOOK OVER IN HER DIRECTION, BRIEFLY FORGETTING SHE WAS EVEN HERE. "I DON'T KNOW. IT'S CRAZY BECAUSE YESTERDAY, HE SAW ME IN MY NOT-AT-ALL CARING BAG AND TODAY, WITH MY WORK CLOTHES. SO, I WANT TO SHOW HIM THAT I HAVE STYLE, BUT I

DON'T WANT TO BE OVERDRESSED OR TOO

COMFORTABLE."

"GIRL, YOU ALREADY MADE AN IMPRESSION. HE

WOULDN'T BE BACK

IF YOU DIDN'T."

"YEAH, BUT HE'S TAKING ME AROUND SOME OF HIS

FRIENDS, WHO I DON'T KNOW ANYTHING ABOUT."

"I WOULDN'T GO SO FAR AS TO SAY THAT," KENDLE

REMARKS.

"YOU TWO LOST ME," ADMITS TOYA AND KENDLE

GIVES THE ALL TOO FAMILIAR LOOK OF EMPATHY.

"WHEN I MET CHRIS," I EXPLAIN, "HE WAS WITH

THIS SEXY ASS DUDE. IT JUST SO HAPPENED THAT CHRIS

WAS THE ONE TO COME AT ME."

"AT YOU, IN YOU, ON YOU, WHATEVER, IT'S YOUR

STORY, BUT LET'S NOT FORGET ABOUT THE FACTS HERE,

SHALL WE?" SINGS KENDLE.

MORE

I SLIGHTLY BOP HER UPSIDE HER HEAD AND WE LAUGH. TOYA GRUNTS, OBVIOUSLY NOT GETTING THE PUNCH LINE. OUR CONVERSATION STEERS OFF INTO SEVERAL OTHERS, AS WE ENJOY SOME MUCH HEEDED GIRL TIME. THE THREE OF US HAS BEEN WRAPPED UP IN OUR OWN LIVES SO MUCH THAT EVEN THOUGH THROUGH PASSING, I SEE AND SPEAK WITH 'TOYA AND SPEAK TO KENDLE ON A DAILY BASIS, ON THE PHONE, WE RARELY HAD THE CHANCE TO JUST CHILL AND HANG OUT.

THE REFRESHINGNESS OF OUR FEMALE BONDING WAS SO ENVELOPING, INCLUDING THE TWO OF THEM SEEMINGLY TRUELY BEGINNING TO HIT IT OFF, I LOSE TRACK OF TIME.

SALEM WALKS IN EMPTY HANDEDLY AND I ASK HIM, "WHAT HAPPENED?"

"SHIT, I'M HUNGRY. MAKE ME SOMETHING TO EAT."

"BOY, YOU BETTER GET OUT OF HERE - I GOT LIKE," I PULL OUT MY CELL. "FUCK!" I CURSE AT MYSELF.

MORE

"WHAT?" KENDLE REFLEXIVELY MOVES HER HEAD, CHECKING HER HAIR.

"CHRIS'LL BE HERE IN 15 AND I DIDN'T EVEN SHOWER YET."

"UP, WELL I GUESS THAT SOLVES THAT. YOU'RE NOT GOING OUT." SALEEM ATTEMPTS TO DICTATE.

"WATCH ME." I MOVE TOWARDS HIM BUT HE BLOCKS MY BEDROOM DOOR.

"MOVE BOY," I TELL HIM AND HIS USELESS TACTIC.

"WHAT YOU JUST GONNA LEAVE WHEN YOU KNOW WE GOT TO FIND CHUCK? AND, I'M HUNGRY ON TOP OF THAT."

"*YOU* GOT TO FIND DADDY AND *YOU* GOT MONEY, GO TO THE STORE. NOW, MOVE," I TELL HIM AS AGITATION GROWS IN MY VOICE.

"WHERE YOU GOING? WHAT TIME YOU COMING BACK? YOU GOING WITH DUDE?"

MORE

"1...," I COUNT.

"YOU GOING BY YOURSELF?" HE TURNS TO KENDLE, "YOU GOING WITH HER, RIGHT?"

"2"

"SO, YOU EXPECT ME TO LET YOU WALK OUT OF HERE WITH SOMEONE WHO I DON'T KNOW ANYTHING ABOUT, OR WHERE YOU'RE GOING?"

SALEEM STUMBLES BACK A FEW STEPS IN REACTION TO ME PUSHING HIM.

"I TOLD YOU TO MOVE DIDN'T I?" I WALK PAST HIM CONTINUING "I'M GROWN. IF YOU REALLY WANT TO KNOW WHERE I'M GOING, USE YOUR GPS ON YOUR PHONE TO SEE WHERE I'M AT. ISN'T THAT WHY YOU GOT IT IN THE FIRST PLACE?" I SLAM THE BATHROOM DOOR BEHIND ME, QUICKLY STRIP AND GET INTO THE SHOWER.

CHAPTER 5

CALLING OUT AFTER KENDLE WISHES ME GOOD LUCK, I LET HER KNOW THAT I WOULD CALL HER TOMORROW. I APPROACH CHRIS' CAR AND NOTICE THAT EVEN WITH WEDGES, STANDING IN FRONT OF HIS 5'9 FRAME, I'M STILL AN INCH SHORTER THAN HIM.

"GOOD EVENING," HE GREETS IN HIS NORMAL IMMACULATE MANNER. "HEY," I REPLY, TUGGING ON MY BLOUSE, AS IF TO STRAIGHTEN IT LOOKING OVER HIS OUTFIT, I WAS GLAD I WAS NOT OVERDRESSED AS WE BOTH WERE WEARING JEANS.

"NO NEED. YOU'RE BEAUTIFUL," HE REMARKS AS HE OPENS THE DOOR FOR ME.

THE CONVERSATION ON OUR WAY WAS FAINT, SO I WAS PRIVILEGED TO LET MY MIND WANDER. WHEN WE PARK, I FINALLY PUSH MY MORE PRESSING THOUGHTS ASIDE, TURN TO HIM AND FOCUS ON HAVING A GOOD TIME.

MORE

"HOW ARE YOU?" HE ASKS.

"IT'S NOTHING, FAMILY STUFF." I SAY DISMISSIVELY. "NOTHING EVERYBODY ELSE DOESN'T GO…" I STOP SHORT, "I AM SO SORRY. I DIDN'T MEAN, I…," HE HOLDS HIS HANDS UP TO STOP ME FROM SPEAKING.

"NO NEED TO APOLOGIZE. YOU HAVE THINGS ON YOUR MIND. BESIDES, YOUR MEANING HAD NO ILL INTENTIONS. I CAN'T FAULT YOU FOR THAT. WOULD YOU LIKE TO SPEAK ABOUT IT? I MAY NOT HAVE ANY FAMILY CURRENTLY, BUT I

PLAN TO. I'VE ALSO, HAD MY FAIR SHARE OF FAMILY DRAMA."

IS HE ONLY SAYING THAT TO MAKE ME FEEL BETTER, OR DOES HE REALLY WANT TO KNOW? WOULD IT BE SELFISH OF ME TO SIT HERE AND BLABBER ON ABOUT MY FAMILY, WHEN HE DOESN'T HAVE ANY?

HE CONTINUES, "WOULD IT HELP IF I TOLD YOU THAT I'VE ALREADY SPOKEN WITH YOUR BROTHER?"

MORE

"WHAT?!" I EXCLAIM. "OH, LORD. I AM SO EMBARRASSED, WHAT DID HE SAY?"

"RELAX, WOULD YOU. YOUR BROTHERS A CHARACTER, NONETHELESS. THE CONVERSATION WE HAD WAS INTERESTING, TO SAY THE LEAST." CHRIS GIVES ME THE DETAILS OF THEIR CONVERSATION AS WE EXIT THE CAR.

RECOGNIZING THE NEIGHBORHOOD AS WE CROSS THE STREET, I HEAR MUSIC AND ASK, "THE PARTY'S AT YOUR HOUSE?"

"WHAT CAN I SAY?" HE RESPONDS. "ANY BEGINNING ARTIST IS A STARVING ARTIST."

ENTERING THE HOUSE, I CLOSE THE DOOR BEHIND ME AND TAKE A LOOK AROUND. GROUPS OF THREE TO FIVE PEOPLE ARE AMONG THEMSELVES CHATTING, MEN AND WOMEN OF VARYING AGES AND RACES.

"WOULD YOU LIKE A DRINK?"

MORE

I DECLINE CHRIS' REQUEST - HE PLACES HIS PALM ON THE SMALL OF MY BACK AS WE WALK TO THE FIRST GROUP OF PEOPLE. HE MAKES INTRODUCTIONS AROUND AND THEY GIVE BACK INTO THEIR PRIOR CONVERSATION OF HOW TO BETTER ACCOMMODATE AN ARTIST WITH SPECIAL NEEDS.

WE MAKE ROUNDS AROUND THE ROOM WHERE THE CONVERSATIONS WERE CENTRAL TO THE ARTS BUT IN DIFFERENT ASPECTS. I WAS SURPRISED AT THE MANY JOBS THIS GROUP HELD. FROM ART TEACHERS, TO WRITERS, POETS, AN AFRICAN ARTS STUDENT. JUST AS WE WERE BREAKING AWAY FROM THE LAST GROUP, IT WAS BROUGHT UP OF HOW THE ART WORLD IS DYING OFF BECAUSE YOUTH IS NO LONGER INTERESTED. I JUMPED RIGHT INTO THE HEATED DEBATE WITH THE ARGUMENT OF KIDS TODAY NOT HAVING THE OPPORTUNITIES TO *DISCOVER* THEIR INTEREST IN THE ARTS DUE TO THE LACK OF FUNDING TO NEIGHBORHOOD SCHOOLS AND

MORE

ULTIMATELY, THE ARTS BEING CUT FROM THE CURRICULUMS.

"IF THAT BE THE CASE, WHY DOESN'T PEOPLE SPEAK UP ON THE MATTER?" COUNTERS ONE IN A SUIT.

"AS FOR THE KIDS, FOR ONE, THEY'RE JUST THAT. KIDS. TO THEM, THEY DON'T KNOW ANY BETTER. IT'S JUST ANOTHER CLASS THAT THEY DON'T HAVE TO TAKE. SECONDLY, IF ARTS AREN'T EXPOSED TO THE KIDS, SO THAT THEY CAN LEARN AND DEVELOP INTEREST, HOW WILL THEIR PARENTS KNOW?"

WE EXCHANGE THOUGHTS, BACK AND FORTH, FOR A WHILE UNTIL HE CONFESSES IT WAS TIME FOR HIM TO LEAVE. HE THANKED ME FOR OUR CONVERSATION AND, ONCE AGAIN, CONGRATULATED CHRIS.

TO CHRIS, I PROUDLY PROFESS WITH A BEAMING FACE, I ASK, "WHAT?"

"YOU ARE SO PASSIONATE IN WHAT YOU BELIEVE. IT'S SURPRISING TO ME THAT YOU HAVEN'T TAKEN UP A PROFESSION IN THE ARTS."

"I DO LOVE TO DANCE. BUT HEY, THAT'S LIFE."

"WELL, IT LOOKS LIKE YOU JUST MIGHT GET YOUR CHANCE TO LOVE AGAIN," HE STATES.

I LOOK AROUND THE ROOM, DODGING WHATEVER MEANING HE MEANT AND MOST OF THE PEOPLE, WHO WE TALKED TO BEFORE, WERE REPLACED BY NEWCOMERS. HEADING OUR WAY WAS A FACE I REMEMBERED.

"I DON 'T BELIEVE YOU TWO HAVE BEEN FORMALLY INTRODUCED. YANI THIS IS C-NOTE. C-NOTE, YANI."

"S'UP." C-NOTE, THE FRIEND FROM THE DENTIST OFFICE, SAYS, SERIOUSLY? "HI," I SAY SHEEPISHLY, THE TINGLING SENSATION BEGIN AGAIN.

"C-NOTE, GO AHEAD AND SET-UP," CHRIS TELLS HIM.

"AIGHT, TIME TO TAKE THIS JOINT UP A NOTCH."

AFTER HE WALKS AWAY, I MAKE NOTE OF HOW THEY ARE FROM TWO DIFFERENT WORLDS. "SO HOW DID YOU TWO BECOME FRIENDS?"

CHRIS SHRUGS HIS SHOULDERS. "IT HAPPENS." HE BEGINS TELLING ME THE STORY AS WE HEAD FOR THE KITCHEN, I GRAB A SODA. GROWING UP HE WAS TYPICAL FOUR-EYED, CHUBBY BOOKWORM. ONE DAY, WHEN HE WAS IN THE FIFTH GRADE, THIS GROUP OF GUYS BEGIN BULLYING HIM. C-NOTE STOOD UP TO THE GROUP OF BULLIES AND TOLD THEM THAT IF THEY DIDN'T LEAVE HIS FRIEND ALONE, THAT HE WOULD GO GET A GROUP OF HIS FRIENDS. LONG STORY SHORT, C-NOTE FRIENDS WERE NOT THE TYPE TO PLAY WITH. CHRIS NEVER HAD A PROBLEM WITH THAT GROUP AGAIN, BUT JUST IN CASE, C-NOTE TAUGHT HIM HOW TO FEND FOR HIMSELF. ONLY

MORE

UNTIL RECENTLY, HAS CHRIS BEEN ABLE TO PAY C-NOTE

BACK VIA CERTAIN CONNECTIONS. FOR INSTANCE, CHRIS

LANDED C-NOTE WITH THE HOTTEST CLUB IN THE TRI-

STATE AREA AS THEIR MAIN D.J.

NO LONGER TO RESIST THE TEMPTATION OF THE

PUMPING MUSIC MIXED BY D.J. C-NOTE, AS HE CALLS

REPEATEDLY OVER THE MICROPHONE, I GRAB CHRIS'S

HAND AND LEAD HIM TO THE DANCE FLOOR, IN THE

MIDDLE OF THE BASEMENT, WHERE THE PARTY HAS

MOVED TO. WE DANCE METICULOUSLY, BODIES

INTERTWINING, RUBBING AND GRINDING ON EACH

OTHER. HIT AFTER HIT WAS BEING PLAYED, YET, NEITHER

ONE OF US LET UP.

OUR FAIR EXCHANGE OF DEVOTIONAL ATTENTION

WAS INTERRUPTED AS THE D.J. CLAIMED CHRIS NEEDED

TO MAKE A STORE RUN. I ASSURED CHRIS THAT I WOULD

BE ALRIGHT IN HIS ABSENCE - WHAT I WASN'T TOO FINE

WITH OR RATHER CONFUSED ABOUT WAS HIM TELLING

ME TO BE CAREFUL. I WATCH AS HE DISAPPEARS UP THE

MORE

STAIRS, THINKING, "WHAT IN THE WORLD COULD HE HAVE MEANT?!" INSTEAD OF TRYING TO FIGURE IT OUT, I PUSH IT ASIDE AND FOCUS ON HAVING A GOOD TIME.

BOBBING MY HEAD TO THE MUSIC, I REFLEXIVELY JUMP AT A TAP ON MY SHOULDER. I TURN AND THERE'S D.J. C-NOTE STANDING TO MY LEFT.

"SUP, SHORTIE?"

"HEY, I SEE YOU KNOW WHAT YOU ARE DOING OVER THERE, YOU GOT EVERYONE IN HERE MOVING," I COMPLIMENT HIM.

"YEAH, I SEE THAT," HE SAYS, LOOKING ME UP AND DOWN. "THAT'S WHAT I DO. KEEP 'EM ON THEIR FEETS WITH THE BEATS, AND YOU KNOW THEY'RE HAPPY."

"THAT'S A DECENT WAY OF LOOKING AT IT."

"ARE YOU HAPPY?" HE ASKS ME.

"YUP, SO FAR, SO GOOD."

MORE

"IF NOT, LET ME KNOW. I'D HATE TO SEE A FROWN ON THAT SEXY LIL FACE OF YOURS," HE REPLIES, ADDING THE EXTRA EFFECT OF LICKING HIS LIPS. "I KNOW YOU LIKE ME,"

"WHA-" I STAMMER AT HIS BOLD STATEMENT.

CHEESING, HE CONTINUES, "YEA, I KNO, SPEECHLESS. LISTEN, LET ME ASK YOU A QUESTION. WHO WAS YOU WAVING TO COME FOLLOW YOU THE OTHER DAY?"

"DOES IT MATTER?"

"HELL, YEAH IT MATTERS."

"THEN, WHY DIDN'T YOU COME INSTEAD OF CHRIS?"

"BECAUSE HE MY MANS, NOM SAYIN'. I MEAN LOOK AT ME, I CAN GET ANY GIRL I WANT."

"BOY PLEASE," I FLUSH AS I START TO GET TURNED OFF FROM HIM.

MORE

I TURN MY HEAD AWAY, YET QUICKLY SNAP IT BACK AT THE FEEL OF SOMEONE IN MY PERSONAL SPACE, I LOOK INTO C-NOTE'S EYES AS HE REMOVES A FEW STRANDS OF HAIR FROM MY FACE.

HE SAYS, "I'M BEGINNING TO THINK I MAY HAVE MADE A MISTAKE, WHICH I DON'T EVER DO." HE STEPS CLOSER, SO CLOSE, WE NOW FEEL EACH OTHER'S BREATH ON OUR SKINS. "I JUST MIGHT HAVE TO RECTIFY IT." AND HE WINKS. WITH A DUMBFOUNDED LOOK, HE ASKS, "DID I JUST SAY 'RECTIFY'? DAMN, I BEEN HANGING WITH THIS DUDE TOO LONG. I'M STARTING TO SOUND LIKE HIM."

THAT COULDN'T HURT, I THINK TO MYSELF.

"YO, LISTEN," HE SAYS. "I GOTTA GET BACK TO MY BOOTH BEFORE THIS TRACK ENDS. IF YOU EVER NEED ANYTHING YOU ALREADY KNO' WHO TO CALL." AND HE HANDS ME HIS BUSINESS CARD.

NOT LIKELY, SEEING AS THOUGH MY BIRTHDAY'S IN DECEMBER- I TAKE IT JUST TO BE POLITE. AS I DO, I

MORE

TUNE IN MORE CLOSELY TO THE TATTOOS ABOVE HIS EYEBROWS, "TRUE BLOOD." C-NOTE WALKS AWAY BEFORE I HAD A CHANCE TO ASK HIM WHAT IT MEANT. WHEN CHRIS GETS BACK, I THOUGHT ABOUT ASKING HIM, BUT FIGURED IF I ASKED HIM THAT THAN I'D HAVE TO TELL HIM ABOUT THE WHOLE THING. WAY TOO MUCH DRAMA, FOR JUST STARTING THINGS OFF. I DAMN SURE DON 'T GOT ANY TIME FOR THAT, NOR AM I TRYING TO RUIN HIS DAY.

HE DROPS ME OFF AT HOME JUST AFTER THREE, NOT CHOOSING TO SPEND THE NIGHT JUST YET. UNLIKE THE FIRST GROUP, HE WAS WEARY OF THE SECOND UNLESS ABSOLUTELY NECESSARY.

CHAPTER 6

I MADE SALEEM GIVE ME MONEY, OUT OF WHAT HE HAD STASHED, FOR HIS CAR NOTE. IT'S NOT LIKE HE

WASN'T JUST GOING TO GO TAKE IT FROM SOMEBODY ELSE ANYWAY. AFTER HE BROUGHT ME BACK FROM THE MARKET, I WAS HAPPY TO HAVE SOME PEACE AND QUIET WHILE HE CONTINUES HIS SEARCH FOR OUR FATHER. I SHOULD'VE JUST TAKEN THE BUS AS MUCH AS HE COMPLAINED OF "BUYING THE WHOLE DAMN STORE." IF HE DIDN'T EAT SO MUCH, HE WOULDN'T HAVE A PROBLEM.

ON TOP OF THAT, WHAT WOULD KUERON SAY, COMING HOME WITHOUT A WELCOME HOME PARTY? LET ALONE, NO FOOD BEING IN THE HOUSE? HE'D FLIP, THAT'S WHAT. KUERON'S BEEN GONE NEARLY TEN YEARS AND I CAN'T EVEN IMAGINE HOW MUCH HE HAS CHANGED. BUT THE ONE THING THAT HASN'T, I'M SURE IS THE FACT OF HIM BEING A HARD ASS. SEE, WHEN I WAS FIVE, MY MOM WALKED OUT ON US DUE TO MY FATHER USING DRUGS. SHORTLY THEREAFTER,
HE LOST HIS JOB AND AT TWELVE, KUERON QUICKLY FILLED HIS SHOES. IT WASN'T A BIG DEAL FOR ME AS I

MORE

THOUGHT THAT IT WAS NORMAL; I DIDN'T KNOW ANYTHING OTHER THAN KUE GIVING US LUNCH MONEY OR PAYING FOR SALEEM'S AND MY SCHOOL CLOTHES.

IN MIDDLE SCHOOL, WHEN LEEM AND I REACHED PUBERTY AT THE

SAME TIME, EVERYTHING CHANGED. IF IT WASN'T EVERY DAY, IT MOST CERTAINLY EVERY OTHER DAY I WOULD BE PRYING THE TWO OF THEM APART OVER THE SAME THING; SALEEM HAVING FRIENDS OR A GIRL OVER AND NOT LISTENING TO KUE. SALEEM'S INEVITABLE RESPONSE BEING THAT KUE WAS NOT HIS FATHER. THANKFULLY, IT ONLY LASTED ROUGHLY A YEAR, RIGHT AROUND THE TIME KUE STARTED TEACHING SALEEM THE TRICKS OF HIS TRADE.

BY THE TIME SALEEM REACHED HIGH SCHOOL, HE HAD PERFECTED HIS OWN METHOD AND KEPT HIS POCKET AND HIS CLOSET FULL. IT WASN 'T ANYTHING FOR ME TO GET ANYTHING FOR ME TO GET ANYTHING I

WANTED. MONEY WAS JUST READILY AVAILABLE. TO WHICH ONLY LASTED A YEAR WHEN KUE CAUGHT A CASE. HE TOOK A FOUR TO EIGHT YEAR DEAL RATHER THAN TAKING IT TO TRIAL AND POSSIBLY GETTING MORE TIME. SALEEM WAS MORE UPSET THAN ANYONE, I GUESS BECAUSE HE WASN'T READY TO TAKE THE FAMILIES REIGNS. THE MEN IN MY FAMILY JUST HAPPENS TO HAVE THE RESPONSIBILITIES DROPPED ON THEIR SHOULDERS, AT SUCH A YOUNG AGE, WHETHER THEY WANT THEM OR NOT. GOOD THING THEY WERE CAPABLE OF HANDLING THEM.

SALEEM WASN'T AS GOOD AT REMEMBERING THE NECESSITIES LIKE KUE. HECK, I STILL HAVE TO PRIORITIZE HIS MONEY FOR HIM, BUT ATLEAST SALEEM BROUGHT IN ENOUGH MONEY TO WHERE WE LIVED COMFORTABLY UNTIL I STARTED PULLING MY OWN WEIGHT.

"YANI! YO, YANI!" I HEAR.

WHAT IN THE WORLD COULD IT BE THIS TIME, I WONDER COMING DOWN THE STAIRS.

"YANI," SALEEM SHOUTS.

"STOP HOLLERING. I'M COMING, DAG. WAIT A MINUTE." WHEN I GET

TO THE BOTTOM OF THE STEPS, I HUFF, "WHAT?"

"GET THIS TRIFLING NIGGA." AND SALEEM PUSHES OFF HIM A DUSTY HOBO LOOKING OLDER MAN.

GETTING A CLOSER LOOK, I CAN'T BELIEVE WHAT I SEE FALLING TO THE FLOOR AS SALEEM LETS GO HIS GRIP. IN THE FIFTEEN YEARS SINCE HE FIRST TOOK A HIT, MY FATHER HAS NEVER LOOKED THIS BAD. FROM THE FLOOR, THE BAG OF BONES IN WEATHERED CLOTHING LOOKS UP TO ME WITH EYES AND CHEEK AS THE ONLY THINGS BARRING ANY TYPE OF RESEMBLANCE.

HE COUGHS, "I DON'T OWE YOU ANY MONEY TOO, DO I?"

MORE

Saleem scoffs, "That would be a start."

I walk over and help my father to his feet. "Saleem, please, don't start."

"Naw, fuck that. He gotta come up with something."

Walking to the staircase, I ask, "And where is he supposed to come up with something?"

"Work, or something. He manages to get his drugs. Why not something for us?"

"Just like you work, hunh Leem?" Reminding him that he doesn't have a real job. Never did. "And besides, when was the last time you needed for anything anyway?"

"I need stuff all the time, what you talking about?!"

"We're not kids anymore Saleem. There's a difference between a *WANT* and a *NEED*. Now bring

More

ME UP A TRASH BAG SO I CAN THROW AWAY DADDY'S FUNKY ASS CLOTHES."

I HEAR SALEEM MUMBLE SOMETHING ABOUT NOT HAVING A FATHER. AS I HELP OUR FATHER UP THE STEPS, I JUST SHAKE MY HEAD. THAT'S JUST SOMETHING I DO NOT FEEL LIKE GETTING INTO. I DEFINITELY DON'T HAVE TIME FOR IT.

I SCRUBBED UNTIL MY ARMS WERE SORE, BUT HE STILL GAVE OFF A FAINT ODOR. NOT OF SWEAT, MUSK, OR RAW ONIONS, BUT SOMETHING OF DECAY. I TAKE HIM OUT, DRY HIM OFF AND DRAIN THE TUB. "THIS IS GOING TO BE A ROUGH RIDE," I TELL MYSELF AS I WITNESS THE DISTINCTIVE DIRT RING CIRCLING THE INNER WALLS OF THE TUB.

I BEGIN TO MAKE DINNER FOR THE TWO OF US, NOT A LOT, BUT I'VE BEEN DOWN THIS ROAD WITH HIM PRIOR; ONE TOO MANY, IF I DO SAY SO MYSELF. THINKING IT WAS

MORE

STATIC FROM MY STEREO BLASTING, I GO CHECK ON A

CLICKING NOISE.

NOTICING DADDY TRYING TO CLIMB OUT OF THE

PARTIALLY OPENED WINDOW, I ASK, "WHAT, THE DOOR

DOESN'T WORK?"

"WHAT'S THAT, SOME SORT OF TRICK DOOR?" HE

ASKS REFERRING TO THE DOUBLE KEY DEADBOLT

LOCKS.

"GOING SOMEWHERE?" AND I POINT TO THE DVD

PLAYER HE MISERABLY TRIES TO HIDE BEHIND HIS BACK.

"UH, YEAH, SEE, WHAT HAD HAPPENED WAS, UH?

SON-OF-A- GUN! NOW, WHAT WAS I SAYING?"

"I GOT SOMETHING FOR YOU?" I SAY WALKING

INTO THE KITCHEN, HOPING HE'D TAKE THE BAIT. MY

NERVES WERE CALMED AS HE DOES BECAUSE I KNOW I

WOULD HAVE HAD TO HEAR SALEEM'S MOUTH ABOUT

THE BRAND-NEW DVD PLAYER BEING MISSING. "HAVE A

SEAT." FIXING HIM A PLATE, I KEEP ONE EYE ON HIM AS I ASK, "SO, WHERE HAVE YOU BEEN?"

THE SHAKING OF HIS LEG QUICKENS. "AROUND."

I DECIDE NOT TO PUSH HIM TO HARD JUST YET.

HE ASKS, "YOU GOT A LITTLE SOMETHING FOR ME, RIGHT?"

DISAPPOINTMENT MASKS HIS FACE AS I SIT HIS PLATE IN FRONT OF HIM. HIS GLASS OF JUICE AND 16 oz BEER SEEMED TO INTEREST HIM. ONLY AFTER ADDING TO SPOONFULS OF SUGAR TO 'THE GLASS OF JUICE, DID HE DOWN IT.

KNOWING THAT THERE HAS TO BE A PART OF THE MAN I ONCE KNEW AS MY LOVING FATHER INSIDE, I SIT DOWN ACROSS FROM HIM AND TRY TO FIGURE OUT. "WHAT YOU'RE NOT HUNGRY?"

"MAYBE LATER," HE ANSWERED, LOOKING AROUND THE KITCHEN. I'M SURE HE HAD OTHER THINGS ON HIS MIND THAN HURTING MY FEELINGS.

"REMEMBER WHEN YOU USED TO TAKE ME TO DANCE PRACTICE?"

"YOU STILL GO?"

"NO, I DON'T THINK THAT PLACE IS EVEN OPEN ANYMORE." I PUT A SPOONFUL OF CORN IN MY MOUTH TRYING TO FIGURE OUT HOW TO PULL HIM OUT OF HIS OWN LITTLE WORLD. "HOW WOULD YOU LIKE TO SEE KUE?"

HIS FACE CONTORTS, HE GETS UP AND I NEARLY KNOCK THE TABLE OVER, RUNNING TO CATCH HIM. "WHAT'S WRONG?" I ASK, STANDING IN FRONT OF HIM.

"WHY ARE YOU DOING THIS TO ME?"

"DOING WHAT?" I RESPOND TO HIS ACCUSATION.

MORE

"HAVEN'T YOU DONE ENOUGH? LET ME GO, JUST LET ME GO BE IN PEACE."

"I KNOW THAT HE WILL WANT TO SEE YOU."

"NO, HE WON'T."

"I'M GLAD I SAW YOU."

"WHY? TELL ME WHY. I HAVEN'T DONE YOU NO GOOD. I'M OUT. I STARE AT HIS BACK AS HE, AGAIN, TRIES TO OPEN THE FRONT DOOR WITHOUT THE KEYS.

MY RESPONSE TO HIS QUESTION BEING, "BECAUSE I ONLY HAVE ONE FATHER."

HIS HEAD TILTS FORWARD AND I WAS SURE I WAS STARTING TO GET THROUGH. THAT WAS UNTIL THAT ALL TOO FAMILIAR SOUND WAS FOLLOWED BY THE SIGHT AND STENCH OF VOMIT.

CHAPTER 7

MORE

THE FOLLOWING DAY, KENDLE CAME OVER TO HELP ME GET READY FOR THE PARTY. I TRIED TO HELP HER COOK, BUT BETWEEN TAKING CARE OF MY FATHER AND TRACKING DOWN KUE'S HOMIES, WHICH MOST DIDN'T HAVE THE SAME NUMBER, KENDLE TOLD ME JUST TO GET OUT OF HER WAY. SHOOT, I WAS JUST GLAD I HAD THE HELP. SALEEM BEEN IN AND OUT ALL DAY STASHING MONEY, LEAVING TOYA MOSTLY TO MY DISPOSAL. SHE CERTAINLY DIDN'T HAVE A PROBLEM GOING AROUND THE NEIGHBORHOOD SPREADING THE WORD. I GUESS SHE WAS JUST HAPPY TO HAVE SOMETHING TO DO.

BY NIGHTFALL, EVERYTHING SEEMED TO BE DONE, FOR THE MOST PART, ASIDE FROM WARMING THINGS UP TOMORROW. KENDLE COMES AND JOINS ME IN MY ROOM JUST AS I WAS FINISHING THE LAST OF MY PHONE CALLS.

SHE POPS IN A MOVIE SAYING, "UGH, I THINK I DID MORE WORK HERE THAN AT MY REAL JOB."

"I DIDN'T KNOW ANSWERING PHONES AT THE PAPER, WAS WORK," I COUNTER JOKINGLY.

"WELL, IF YOU STOP CALLING ME AT WORK, THEN MAYBE I WILL BE ABLE TO GET SOME WORK DONE."

OUR LAUGHTER WAS INTERRUPTED BY A THUD IN THE NEXT ROOM. I RUN IN TO CHECK ON MY FATHER WHO WAS LYING ON THE FLOOR SHAKING. I CHECK HIM TO SEE WHAT WAS GOING ON, AND HIS WHOLE BODY WAS ICE COLD. I YELL TO KENDLE TO RUN ME A HOT BATH AS I GRAB AN EXTRA BLANKET FROM THE CLOSET. I WRAP IT, AND THE ONE FROM HIS BED, AROUND HIM AS I GET HIM BACK INTO BED.

ON THE WAY DOWN THE STEPS, TO MAKE SOME HOT TEA AND SOUP, KENDLE TELLS ME SHE'LL HELP HIM IN THE TUB. I BUMP MY HEAD ON THE BOTTOM OF THE SINK, TRYING TO FIND A POT I WAS LOOKING FOR, WHEN MY CELL PHONE RINGS.

"HEY, MR. ROBINSON."

"GOOD EVENING. I'M GLAD TO KNOW MY PRESENCE HASN 'T BEEN FORGOTTEN."

"YEAH, I'M SORRY." I SIGH. "I BEEN BUSY WITH SOME FAMILY STUFF, BUT I DEFINITELY HAVEN'T FORGOTTEN ABOUT YOU."

"IS EVERYTHING ALL RIGHT?"

"EVERYTHING'S GOOD. WE JUST GETTING READY FOR MY BROTHER TO COME HOME TOMORROW."

"IS THERE ANYTHING THAT I COULD HELP YOU WITH?" I SET THE POT OF WATER TO BOIL. "YOU'RE KEEPING ME FROM STRESSING RIGHT NOW," I ADMIT.

"IS THAT SO?"

I AGREE.

"FOR FUTURE REFERENCE, YOU DO KNOW THAT THERE ARE OTHER WAYS TO REDUCE STRESS?" HE ASKS.

"OH REALLY," I INQUIRE SARCASTICALLY, MY SMILE RADIATING THROUGH MY VOICE. "HOW SO?"

More

WE BEGIN OUR FIRST PHONE SEX SESSION AS I RUN UP TO CHECK ON MY FATHER. WITH EVERYTHING LOOKING FINE, HIS SHIVERING SLOWED CONSIDERABLY, I RETURN TO THE KITCHEN. IT WAS FIVE MINUTES LATER WHEN CHRIS CLIMAXED AND THE CONVERSATION MOVED ON.

I HAD JUST INVITED HIM TO THE PARTY AND WAS TELLING HIM WHAT TYPE OF FOOD I WAS SERVING WHEN AN AWFUL RACKET, RICOCHETING THROUGH THE HOUSE. AFTER INVESTIGATING, I TOLD CHRIS I WOULD HAVE TO CALL HIM BACK. AT THE BOTTOM OF THE STEPS LIES MY NAKED, SHIVERING FATHER IN A PILE OF VOMIT THAT LEFT A TRAIL BEHIND HIM.

ANOTHER LONG NIGHT OF REHABILITATION LEFT ME WITH LITTLE SLEEP. BUT I GET DRESSED FOR WORK. WITH NO OTHER OPTION, TOYA WAS LEFT TO SIT WITH MY FATHER WHILE SALEEM WENT TO PICK UP KUE. I WAS TEMPTED TO CALL OFF, KNOWING HOW INCOMPETENT

MORE

SHE IS, BUT THAT WASN'T AN OPTION. SO, I WENT ON TO WORK, PRAYING FOR THE BEST.

IT WAS JUST ONE OF THOSE DAYS. I DIDN'T GIVE MS. JONES THE SATISFACTION OF GOING WORD FOR WORD WITH HER, SO SHE OPTED TO HAVE ME RUN AROUND WITH HER NEVER ENDING TO DO LIST. GRATEFULLY, MS. ZUICK WAS AT A DOCTORS APPOINTMENT, SO I GOT THE AFTERNOON OFF. THE BLACK IMPALA IN FRONT OF MY DOORSTEP LET ME KNOW SALEEM'S BACK. TAKING A DEEP BREATH, I WALK IN.

IT'S ABSOLUTELY QUIET, NO ONE ON THE FIRST FLOOR AT ALL. I FIND KUE SITTING BEDSIDE, WATCHING OUR FATHER SLEEP. STANDING THERE GETTING A GOOD LOOK AT HIM, HE FINALLY TURNS AROUND AND ALL OF A SUDDEN, A SENSE OF COMFORT COMES OVER ME I HAVEN'T FELT IN A LONG TIME.

HE TAKES' A HOLD OF MY HAND AND LEADS ME TO MY ROOM. ENVELOPED IN HIS ARMS, THAT ARE BIGGER

MORE

THAN I REMEMBER, I CRY. NEVER BEFORE HAS HE, BUT HE ALLOWS ME TO THIS TIME. WHEN WE WERE YOUNGER, HE WOULD TELL ME TO SUCK IT UP. AFTER I FINISH, HE LETS ME GO AND WIPES MY FACE.

"YOU MISSED ME TOO?" HE ASKS.

I SNIFFLE AND NOD MY HEAD.

"I MISSED YOU TOO, LIL G." HE GRIPS ME UP INTO ANOTHER HUG.

"UH, KUE. DON'T NOBODY CALL ME LIL G ANYMORE. IT'S YANI NOW."

LOOKING AT ME STRANGELY, HE ASKS, "WHY NOT?"

"'LIL' G' A BOY NAME."

THINKING ABOUT IT, HE NODS HIS HEAD. "STILL, YOU'LL ALWAYS BE 'LIL' G', TO ME. MY 'LIL' G.'"

I SMILE.

"YOU GOOD NOW?" HE ASKS.

"YUPPER."

"AIGHT THEN, WHAT'S THIS I'M HEARING YOU ROLLING AROUND TOWN WITH A DUDE DON'T NO BODY KNOW?"

FUCKING SALEEM. "YOU'LL MEET HIM TONIGHT," I TELL HIM SHIFTING UNCOMFORTABLY FROM ONE LEG ONTO THE OTHER.

"MM-HMM, WHAT'S BEEN GOING ON ROUND HERE? YA'LL AIN'T BEEN WRITING TO HEAVY THESE PAST COUPLE YEARS."

I TAKE HIM DOWN TO THE KITCHEN, UPDATING HIM AS I BEGIN SETTING UP FOR THE PARTY. COME TO FIND OUT, SALEEM TOLD HIM BITS AND PIECES, BUT IT WAS I WHO GAVE HIM THE DETAILS. BESIDES QUESTIONS CLAIRIFING, WHAT OR WHO I WAS TALKING ABOUT, IT WAS ME WHO WAS DOING MOST OF THE TALKING.

MORE

PULLING OUT SALEEM'S CAR KEYS AS A SIGNAL HE'S GETTING READY TO LEAVE. I LOOK AT THE CLOCK, WE'VE BEEN CATCHING UP FOR NEARLY

FOUR HOURS.

"KUE, PEOPLE'LL START SHOWING UP HERE A SIX, WHERE YOU GOING?" "WELL, I HAVE AN HOUR, NOW DON'T I?" HE DEFLECTS MY QUESTION.

STILL EVASIVE AS EVER. "WHERE'S SALEEM?" I ASK.

"LYING UP WITH THAT CHICK." HE STANDS AND ASKS, "YOU NEED SOMETHING?"

A TEAR PRICKS THE CORNER OF MY EYE, AS I FIGHT THE URGE TO CRY. "NO," I REPLY A MOMENT LATER. IT TOOK ME A MOMENT SIMPLY BECAUSE IT WAS THE SAME RUN DOWN AS JUST BEFORE HE WENT TO JAIL THE LAST TIME.

CHAPTER 8

MORE

KENDLE HAD COME IN SHORTLY AFTER KUE HAD LEFT, GIVING ME A CHANCE TO SHOWER, DRESS, AND STRAIGHTEN UP. BY 6:30, WE HAD A NICE CROWD, BEING AS THOUGH YOU COULDN'T WALK THROUGH THE LIVING ROOM WITHOUT BUMPING INTO SOMEONE.

MR. ROBINSON SHOWED UP, ON TIME, WITH C-NOTE. WE ALL SIT DOWN, ME ON MR. ROBINSONS LAP, TOYA ON SALEEM'S AND KENDLE BETWEEN THE PAIR OF US. I DON'T KNOW HOW MANY TIMES PEOPLE CAME UP TO ME ASKING WHEN WAS KUE ARRIVING TO HIS OWN PARTY, BUT I WAS GETTING TIRED OF IT AND I KNOW SOME PEOPLE WERE GETTING READY TO LEAVE BY THE TIME HE ACTUALLY DID SHOW HIS FACE.

STOPPING A FEW TIMES TALKING TO PEOPLE, HE FINALLY MAKES HIS WAY OVER TO WHERE WE WERE. I HAD ALREADY POINTED KUE OUT TO CHRIS BY THIS TIME

AND I TOOK HIS SEAT AS CHRIS STOOD UP TO SHAKE

KUE'S HAND AS THEY

WALK OFF TO TALK.

KENDLE ASKS, "SALEEM, WHAT HAPPENED TO

YOU?"

THOUGHTLESSLY, WE ALL JOIN IN LOOKING AT

SALEEM.

"WHAT CHU' TALKIN' 'BOUT?" HE ASKS.

"YOUR BROTHER LOOKS *DAMNED* GOOD."

LAUGHING, SALEEM TELLS ME TO GET MY FRIEND,

BUT HE STOPS SHORT WHEN HE NOTICES TOYA ISN'T

LAUGHING.

WE ALL CONTINUE JOKING AROUND TILL MR.

ROBINSON AND KUE RETURNS.

"WHAT'S UP BLOOD?"

C-NOTE STANDS, "WHAT IT BE LIKE?"

I LOOK BACK AND FORTH BETWEEN KUE AND C-NOTE WONDERING WHAT'S GOING ON, NOT DARING TO ASK.

"CHILL BRO, YOU AMONG FAMILY," KUE TELLS HIM.

"WORD?"

KUE NODS HIS HEAD IN MY DIRECTION. "ON MY SIS."

THEY DO SOME SORT OF WEIRD HANDSHAKE I NEVER SAW BEFORE AND CONTINUE ON WITH THE REST OF US LIKE THAT EXCHANGE NEVER EVEN HAPPENED. THE PARTY WAS A HIT. EVERYONE WAS HAVING A GOOD TIME, LAUGHING, JOKING. KENDLE WAS THE FIRST TO GO HOME HAVING TO WORK IN THE MORNING.

AFTER COMING BACK DOWN FROM CHECKING ON MY FATHER, A LOT OF PEOPLE HAD LEFT.

MORE

"EVERYTHING'S FINE. I BELIEVE YOU SHOULD BE PROUD. YOUR PARTY WAS SUCCESSFUL."

"THANKS, CHRIS." I LOOK AROUND AND FIND KUE WITH C-NOTE.

"HE AND HIS GIRLFRIEND LEFT A FEW MOMENTS AGO," CHRIS TELLS ME AFTER I KEPT SEARCHING. I SHAKE MY HEAD, AND HE ASKS, "IS SOMETHING THE MATTER?"

"YOU AMAZE ME, YOU KNOW THAT?"

"THAT SHOULD BE A GOOD THING."

"IT IS," I ASSURE HIM. "I DON'T KNOW HOW YOU KNEW I WAS CHECKING IN ON MY BROTHERS."

"WHY? IF YOU DON'T MIND ME ASKING. THEY'RE BOTH ADULTS AND BY THE LOOKS OF THINGS, THEY CAN DEFINITELY TAKE CARE OF THEMSELVES."

"YOU DON'T KNOW MY BROTHERS."

"CAN WE WALK?" I AGREE. HAND IN HAND, WE WALK THROUGH MY NEIGHBORHOOD. "YOU HAVE A LOT RESTING ON YOUR SHOULDERS," HE REMARKS.

"IT COMES WITH THE TERRITORY. NOTHING I CAN'T HANDLE," I ASSURE HIM.

"AND IS THIS THE TERRITORY YOU SEE FOR YOURSELF?"

"IT'S THE ONLY ONE I KNOW."

"AND IF YOU HAD AN OPPORTUNITY TO COME FROM OUT OF IT?"

MYSTIFIED, I GAZE INTO HIS CHOCOLATE EYES THAT CONTRAST AGAINST HIS PEACH-COLORED FACE. NOT KNOWING THE ANSWER.

CLARIFYING, HE CONTINUES, "THE GENTLEMAN YOU DEBATED WITH AT MY HOUSE THE OTHER NIGHT WAS GARY COMBS, THE SUPERINTENDENT OF THE PHILADELPHIA SCHOOL DISTRICT. HE CALLED ME THIS

MORNING SAYING THAT HE WAS VERY IMPRESSED WITH YOUR POSITION ABOUT TODAYS YOUTH AND THE ARTS. HE WANTS TO SET UP A MEETING WITH YOU IN FRONT OF THE OTHER BOARD MEMBERS STATING THAT IF YOU CAN IMPRESS THEM, JUST AS YOU DID HIM, HE IS SURE YOU'LL BE GUARANTEED A SPOT AMONG THEM AS AN 'AYA' (AMBASSADOR OF THE YOUTH IN ARTS)."

WITH DOUBT CLOUDING MY REASONING AND JUDGEMENT, I ASK, "WHY ME?"

"FOR ONE, YOU'RE YOUNG AND WILL MORE EQUIP IN RELATING TO THE STUDENTS. YOU ARE PASSIONATE ABOUT THE ARTS WHICH MEANS YOU'LL BE BETTER QUALIFIED, THEN A PERSON WHO HAS A DEGREE IN THE ARTS BUT DOESN'T NECESSARILY CARE FOR IT."

"ALL OF THIS IS SO SUDDEN AND NEW TO ME," I EXPLAIN. "I'M NOT SURE IF I'M THE RIGHT PERSON."

STANDING ON THE SIDEWALK IN FRONT OF MY HOUSE, I LOOK INTO HIS FACE AS HE ASSERTS, "YANI,

MORE

THIS IS YOU. NO ONE ELSE CAN FILL THIS POSITION BETTER THAN YOU. WHY DO YOU DOUBT YOURSELF? WHY ARE YOU HOLDING YOURSELF BACK?"

I LOOK BACK TOWARDS MY DOOR AND NOTICE KUE SAYING HIS GOODBYES TO THE LAST OF THE PARTY PEOPLE. I TURN BACK TO CHRIS DIRECTION, EYES FIXATED ON THE GROUND.

HE TAKES A DEEP BREATH BEFORE STATING THAT HE UNDERSTANDS AND ASKS ME TO ATLEAST THINK ABOUT IT. I PROMISE HIM THAT I WILL AND JUST BEFORE HIM AND C-NOTE DRIVE OFF, I GIVE HIM ONE LAST HUG AND KISS.

CHAPTER 9

THE FOLLOWING WEEK, THANKS TO SALEEM STAYING WITH TOYA, KUE TOOK HIS ROOM AND BEGAN

MORE

TAKING CARE OF DADDY, I FINALLY HAD A CHANCE TO REALLY THINK ABOUT MY OPTIONS AND WHERE I WANTED TO GO IN LIFE. I WAS SO FOCUSED, BEFORE, ON JUST SURVIVING AND THE FAMILY, I HAD LEFT ME, MYSELF, OUT OF THE MIX. ONLY TELLING TWO PEOPLE OF THE JOB OPPORTUNITY, MISS ZUICK AND KENDLE, THEY BOTH TOLD ME TO GO FOR IT. I ADMIT, IT IS A GOOD JOB, BUT SOMEHOW, I FEEL LIKE I'LL BE BETRAYING SOMEONE IF I DO; OR, EVEN IF I DON'T.

BEING A FRIDAY, KUE DECIDED TO TAKE EVERYONE OUT. I WAS HOPING I COULD GET MISS ZUICK TO LET ME GO EARLY BUT BEING AS THOUGH SHE WAS SICK THAT ENDED MY HOPES. HONESTLY THOUGH, I DIDN'T MIND, NORMALLY MY AFTERNOONS BE A BREEZE WITH HER USUALLY DOING EVERYTHING HERSELF ANYWAY. PER HER REQUEST, I MADE HER A POT OF VEGETABLE SOUP WITH A WHOLE HEAD OF GARLIC.

SHE WASN'T IN THE MOOD FOR CHIT CHAT TODAY, SO AS I CLEANED HER APARTMENT I SPOKE WITH CHRIS.

MORE

WITH THE VOICE THAT ALWAYS TAKES MY BREATH AWAY, HE ANSWERS THE PHONE EVER SO CONFIDENTLY, "HELLO?"

"HEY."

"HOW ARE YOU?"

"I'M GOOD, WORKING."

"I AM TOO," HE ADMITS. "WELL, NOT NECESSARILY WORK, BUT IN THE MIDDLE OF A PROJECT."

"OH, YEAH, OF WHAT?"

"I CAN'T TELL YOU THAT."

"WHY NOT?" I ASK, SLIGHTLY OFFENDED.

"BECAUSE IT'S FOR YOU."

"FOR ME?"

"ABSOLUTELY, AND JUST THINK, I GOT THE IDEA FOR MY PAINTING FROM THE ZOO."

MORE

MY EGO TAKING ANOTHER BLOW, I ASK, "I REMIND YOU OF AN ANIMAL?"

"NO, YOU ARE TWISTING MY WORDS. YOU INSPIRED ME TO DO A PORTRAIT FOR YOU. I DREW EVEN MORE INSPIRATION WHEN I VISITED THE ZOO, AND THAT'S WHEN MY IDEAS STARTED FALLING INTO PLACE." A SILENCE WAS BROKEN WHEN HE CONTINUED, "WHEN WAS THE LAST TIME YOU VISITED THE ZOO?"

"I DON'T THINK I HAVE EVER BEEN," I CONFESS.

"WHEN DO YOU GET OFF FROM WORK?"

"USUALLY FIVE, BUT I RARELY STAY THAT LATE."

"IS TODAY ONE OF THOSE DAYS?"

"DOUBTFUL, I DIDN'T HAVE TOO MUCH TO DO TODAY. I'M ALMOST DONE."

"WOULD YOU BE DONE, IN SAY FORTY-FIVE MINUTES, WHEN I COME PICK YOU UP?"

MORE

HMM, 3:45. "YEAH, I CAN MANAGE THAT. SO, WHERE ARE WE GOING?"

"WHERE ELSE? TO HELP YOU EXPAND YOUR HORIZONS."

THE ZOO WAS INTERESTING, TO SAY THE LEAST. I HADN'T HAD SUCH A GOOD TIME IN SO LONG, I ALMOST FORGOTTEN WHAT IT FELT LIKE TO BE TREATED SPECIAL. CHRIS HELPED ME TO SEE THAT ANYONE CAN DRAW INSPIRATION FROM JUST ABOUT ANYTHING. I DIDN'T KNOW THAT THEY HAD SUCH AN ARRAY OF WILDLIFE; FROM THE TONS OF ANTS, TO THE LITERAL TONS OF ELEPHANTS. HE WAS SO MOTIVATED TO TRANSFORM WHAT HE HAD EXPERIENCED THERE, ONTO A CANVAS THAT I HAD COME TO THE REALIZATION IF HE HADN'T, I WOULD HAVE BEEN DISAPPOINTED.

~PAGE BREAK~

MORE

"HURRY UP LIL G. I WANNA GET A GOOD SPOT," KUE CALLS OUT TO ME AS I'M HOPPING OUT OF THE SHOWER.

I DON'T KNOW WHY HE'S RUSHING, THE SHOW STARTS AT EIGHT AND IT'S ONLY SEVEN TWENTY. NOT WANTING TO DEAL WITH HIS IMPATIENCE, I ABIDE BY HIS REQUEST AND QUICKLY JUMP INTO THE BACK SEAT WITH KENDLE AND TOYA.

ON OUR WAY, KUE EXPLAINED HE HAD BACKSTAGE PASSES TO THE CONCERT AND WE'D BE ABLE TO CHILL WITH HIS BLOOD BROTHER, ONE OF THE ENTERTAINERS PERFORMING TONIGHT, AND GET TO HANG OUT IN HIS DRESSING ROOM.

WHEN I ASK KUE WHO WAS HE TALKING ABOUT, SALEEM, THINKING IT WAS HIM, HE QUICKLY SAYS, "I AIN'T DOIN NO SHOW."

"WHY DIDN'T YOU STAY IN SCHOOL AGAIN?" KUE ASKS AND THE INSIDE FAMILY JOKE GETS LAUGHS FROM

MORE

EVERYONE. AFTER IT ALL DIED DOWN, KUE ANSWERS MY QUESTION, "CHRIS."

"CHRIS? WHAT CHRIS? MY CHRIS?"

WITH A SMILE THROUGH THE REARVIEW MIRROR, KUE SAYS "WE'LL SEE ABOUT THAT." HE CONTINUES TO RUSH US AS WE MAKE OUR WAY THROUGH THE PARKING LOT OF THE WACHOVIA CENTER, MINUTES TO EIGHT.

BEING AS THOUGH CHRIS WAS THE OPENING ACT, WE COLLECTIVELY DECIDE TO GIVE THE CONCESSION STANDS A RAIN CHECK. PROUD OF BEING IN THE FRONT ROW, JUST TO SEE CHRIS' EXPRESSION WHEN HE SEES ME, BUT CONFUSED AS TO WHY HE DIDN'T MENTION ANYTHING ABOUT IT EARLIER WHEN WE WENT OUT.

WITH TIME TO SPARE, I MEAN, COME ON, WHEN DOES ANYTHING START ON TIME? KUE AND SALEEM DECIDE TO GO GET US ALL SOME SNACKS BY THE TIME THE PERFORMER WALKED ON STAGE, THEY MADE THEIR

MORE

WAY BACK AND I TELL KUE THAT THE PERFORMERS NAME IS C-NOTE, NOT CHRIS.

HE RESPONDS WITH, "THAT'S WHAT THE 'C' STANDS FOR. MM-MM MM, THE ONLY ONE WHO GRADUATED HIGH SCHOOL AND WENT TO TRADE SCHOOL. OUT OF ALL OF US, I THOUGHT YOU WOULD HAVE FIGURED THAT OUT."

POPULAR BEATS FOLLOWED BY ONES I NEVER HEARD BEFORE; C-NOTE SPIT HIS ORIGINAL LYRICS FOR FIVE SONGS. UNIQUE IN HIS OWN STYLE, I GIVE HIM CREDIT FOR, IT SOUNDS OK, BUT AS THE LYRICS, I COULD HAVE DONE WITHOUT.

"F THE BIOTCH, JUST LAY THE PIPE ON HER LIKE A CARD TO A KIOSK." AND "ALL THIS MONEY-MAKING DICK SLINGING MACHINE NEEDS IS A BROAD WHO KNOWS HOW TO COOK CLEAN AND KEEP A BROTHA WELL PLEASED." GRABBING HIS CROTCH TO MAKE SURE YOU CATCH HIS DRIFT. UNFORTUNATELY FOR ME, IT WAS AN UNDESIRED EFFECT.

MORE

BACKSTAGE, I SIT CHATTING WITH TOYA AND KENDLE WHILE THE GUYS DO THEIR THING. KENDLE KEEPS TRYING TO PERSUADE ME, BUT I TOLD HER I'D THINK IT'LL BE TOO WEIRD.

"I'M TELLING YOU, IT'S NOT GOING TO BE WEIRD, WE ALREADY LIKE SISTERS. I'M TRYING TO GET WITH KUE BEFORE SOMEONE ELSE DO. WHY YOU COCK BLOCKING?"

TOYA ADDS, "YOU THINK IT'S WEIRD THAT I'M WITH LEEM?"

"OF COURSE NOT."

"THEN WHY WOULD IT BE WEIRD FOR ME TO GET WITH KUE?" KENDLE ASKS.

"OKAY, IT'S ONLY ONE WAY TO SETTLE THIS." I CALL KUE OVER, AND HE TELLS ME JUST A MINUTE AS SALEEM COMES INSTEAD.

"YOUR BROTHER'S A TRIP. HE STILL AIN'T CHANGE," HE SAYS, SITTING DOWN.

MORE

I ASKED SALEEM WHAT WAS HE TALKING 'BOUT, BUT HE DIDN'T GET A CHANCE TO EXPLAIN AS KUE, HIMSELF, WALKED OVER.

"HEY, KENDLE'S TRYNA GET AT YOU. WHAT'S UP WITH THAT?" I ASK.

LOOKING HER OVER, NONCHALANTLY, HE STATES, "THAT'LL WORK." BENDING DOWN IN FRONT OF ME, WITH THIS 'UP TO NO GOOD LOOK IN HIS EYE', "LISTEN, I NEED YOU TO DO SOMETHING FOR ME THAT'S REALLY IMPORTANT."

"LAY IT ON NICE AND THICK," SALEEM COMMENTS.

KUE SHOOTS HIM A DEATH STARE, WHICH SILENCES HIM.

"WHAT?" I ASK.

KUE ASKS, "YOU KNOW WHAT MY DREAM HAS ALWAYS BEEN RIGHT?"

MORE

"FOR US TO BE HAPPY AND LEAST OF ALL COMFORTABLE."

"TRUE, TRUE," KUE COMMENTS. "BESIDES THAT."

I THINK FOR A MOMENT AND THEN TELL HIM THE TRUTH, "I GOT NOTHING ELSE."

"SOMETHING FUNNY?" HE ASKS A SNICKERING SALEEM. BACK TO ME, KUE SAYS, "LOOK, C-NOTE LIKES YOU, BAD. AND I WANNA GET IN THE MUSIC GAME."

"KUE, I GOTTA MAN."

"YOU JUST TALKING TO DUDE, YANI. I AIN'T ASKING YOU TO MARRY HIM OR SOMETHING."

"NOT YET," SALEEM ADDS.

KUE STANDS UP AND ASKS SALEEM TO SAY IT A LITTLE LOUDER; TO STOP MUMBLING UNDERNEATH OF HIS BREATH. BUT SALEEM KNEW BETTER.

TO DEFER THE TENSION, AS ALWAYS, I ASK KUE, "TALK TO HIM? THAT'S IT? AND HE'LL HOOK YOU UP?"

"THAT'S IT LIL'G," KUE RESPONDS.

AGAINST MY BETTER JUDGEMENT, I SAUNTER OVER AND SIT ON THE COUCH OPPOSITE OF C-NOTE. HE FAILS TO GET A LAUGH FROM ME WITH HIS JOKES. I CAME WITH THE ATTITUDE OF NOT CATCHING THE BAIT, UNLESS I WANTED TO. NEEDLESS TO SAY, I DO LIGHTEN UP AFTER THINKING ABOUT THE WHOLE SITUATION. I'M DOING IT FOR MY BROTHER. IT'S THE LEAST I CAN DO FOR HIM FOR ALL OF THE THINGS HE DID FOR ME OVER THE YEARS. BUT, WILL CHRIS BELIEVE IT AFTER JUST WALKING IN AND SEEING C-NOTE'S HAND ON MY THIGH?

CHAPTER 10

ON THE RIDE TO HIS PLACE, I EXPLAIN THE WHOLE SCENARIO TO HIM, BUT CHRIS DOESN'T SAY A WORD. ONLY AFTER ASKING WOULD I TAKE A RIDE WITH HIM. HE

GETS OUT OF THE CAR, OPENS THE FRONT DOOR OF HIS HOUSE, PICKS ME UP AND CARRIES ME UP THE STAIRS.

LAYING ME ON HIS EXTRA SOFT CALIFORNIA KING, HE DELICATELY KISSES ME ON MY EXPOSED SKIN AS HE UNBUTTONS MY BLOUSE. HE POPS ONE OF BREAST FROM MY BLACK LACE BRA INTO HIS MOUTH, HIS TONGUE FLICKING AROUND MY SENSITIVE NIPPLES. AFTER ALTERNATING FROM LEFT TO RIGHT, HE UNBUTTONS MY PANTS. I LEFT MY WAIST IN THE AIR SO HE CAN PULL OFF MY JEANS AND PANTIES EASIER. MY HIPS ARE HELD IN PLACE, STOPPING MY BODY FROM UNVOLUTARILY JERKING BY THE PLEASURE CHRIS' TONGUE BRINGS. MY LEGS ARE SO TENSE, IF I WAS A SCHOLAR IN LINGUISTICS, I COULDN'T FIND THE RIGHT WORDS TO DESCRIBE IT TO YOU.

PRAYING NO ONE WOULD CALL THE COPS AFTER THE SCREAM I LET OUT, I HEAR CHRIS MAKING THE SOUND OF A STRAW IN AN EMPTY CUP, SLURPING ALL OF MY JUICES. I TELL HIM THAT IT WAS GOOD AND HE

MORE

SHUSHES ME. STANDING, HIS PANTS FALLS TO THE FLOOR. I TAKE IN A SHARP BREATH, STILL NOT USED TO THE SIZE OF HIS PENIS AS IT OPENS UP MY VAGINA. WITH MORE OF A MOMENTUM THEN OUR FIRST TIME, AND NOT THE POUNDING FROM SMALLER ERECTIONS THAT I'M USED TO, CHRIS BEGINS LONG STROKING ME.

"CHR-" HIS TONGUE ENTERS MY MOUTH AND I TASTE MY OWN JUICES, CUTTING ME OFF. WE KISS, WHILE MAKING LOVE AS I LEAVE DELICATE TRAILS ALONG HIS BACK. UNABLE TO THINK BEFORE HIS RIGID JERK, I USE THIS TIME TRY AND FIGURE OUT WHY THIS TIME, AND WITH HIM, SEX IS SO MUCH DIFFERENT.

LEANING UP, BUT NOT PULLING OUT, HE LIFTS ME UP BY HOLDING ME BETWEEN MY SHOULDER BLADES. AS HE SITS DOWN, HE LOWERS ME INTO A STRADDLING POSITION. MY FACE CRINGE, AS HE GOES DEEPER INTO ME. WITH A BITE ON MY NECK, THE PAIN AND THE PLEASURE COINCIDE AS I BEGIN TO ROCK BACK AND FORTH.

MORE

AFTER THE THIRD TIME OF MY JUICES FLOWED, MY MEMORY DOESN'T DEPICT ANYTHING, SO I'M SURE IT'S WHEN WE FELL ASLEEP. I LIFT OFF OF HIS SCULPTED HAIRLESS CHEST TO MARVEL IN HIS EYES.

"GOOD MORNING," HE SAYS RUNNING HIS FINGERS THROUGH MY HAIR.

"MORNING," I SHIFT MY BODY TO WHERE I'M LYING DIRECTLY ON TOP OF HIM AND INSTANTLY FEEL HIM BEGIN TO HARDEN.

HE RAISES HIS EYEBROWS.

"NO, SORRY. I'M STILL SORE FROM LAST NIGHT. BESIDES, IT'S TIME TO TALK."

"SPEAK FREELY," HE SAYS.

"BY THE LOOK ON YOUR FACE LAST NIGHT, I COULD TELL YOU DIDN'T LIKE THE FACT THAT C-NOTE WAS FEELING ME UP."

"ALSO SURPRISED THAT YOU WERE THERE."

MORE

"KUE NEVER TOLD US WHO THE CONCERT WAS FOR," I EXPLAIN.

"WHY DIDN'T YOU TELL ME C-NOTE AND YOU HAD THE SAME NAME?"

"IT HAPPENS, THOUGHT IT WOULD BE LESS CONFUSING THAT WAY."

"SO, WHAT WAS LAST NIGHT ABOUT?"

HE MADE HIS MUSCLE MOVE BETWEEN MY LEGS. "I SHOWED YOU."

AFTER NOT GETTING HIS MEANING, I ASK, "CAN YOU TELL ME?"

"YANI, I'M NOT ONE OF THESE GUYS WHO CREATE FALSE IDENTITIES BECAUSE THEY DISLIKE WHO THEY REALLY ARE. I CAME TO YOU THAT DAY IN THE DENTIST OFFICE BECAUSE I LIKE YOU. NOW, … EVEN MORE SO. WHAT YOU SEE IS WHAT YOU GET WITH ME. AND YOU GOT ALL OF ME."

NOT KNOWING WHAT TO SAY, I DON'T SAY ANYTHING. THAT'S IF YOU DON'T COUNT THE GROWLING IN MY STOMACH.

HE RAISES AN EYEBROW, "BREAKFAST?" AND WE CHUCKLE.

"YES," I SAY ROLLING OFF OF HIM. "PLEASE."

"THERE'S A NEW PACK OF TOOTHBRUSHES UNDER THE SINK." HE LOOKS BACK AT ME AS HE GETS OUT OF BED WITH HIS STATUESQUE BODY. BEFORE HE LEAVES THE ROOM, HE SAYS, "DON'T WORRY ABOUT CLOTHES, WE'LL BUY YOU SOME NEW ONES."

I GET DRESSED IN HIS ABSENCE AND CHECK MY VOICEMAIL. THERE WAS A TWO FOR ONE, LEFT BY SALEEM AND KENDLE SAYING THAT THEY BOTH HAD TO TALK BUT FOR DIFFERENT REASONS. I CALL KENDLE FIRST, NOT WANTING TO DEAL WITH SALEEM AND WHATEVER ISSUE HE HAD. WE SHARED UPDATES OF HOW OUR NIGHTS ENDED, WHICH WERE SIMILAR, BUT NOT

WANTING TO HEAR THE DETAILS OF MY BROTHER, OR OF HOW THE SEX WITH HIM WAS. WE CONTINUED TALKING UNTIL CHRIS APPEARED WITH A TRAY OF FOOD, ENDING THE CALL.

CHRIS AND I MAPPED OUT OUR DAY OVER BREAKFAST, BY WHICH, I WAS SURE I GAINED ATLEAST TEN POUNDS. WHILE LOATHING IN MY SLOTHNESS, HE PRESENTED ME WITH A PORTRAIT STATING THAT HE NEVER CREATED ONE JUST FOR A SINGLE PERSON. THE THREE INTERTWINING BACKDROPS AND ANIMALS ARE REFLECTIVELY EXPLAINED IN A POEM ALONG THE BOTTOM.

STRONG, LIKE THE JAWS

OF A FULL BLOOD PIT BULL

FIERCE LIKE THE LIONESS

IN THE JUNGLE, YOU RULE

STRIKING BEAUTY

MORE

UNMATCHED BY A COBRA

REVITALIZING VENOM

INSTEAD OF, SLUMPING ME OVER

FEELING REFRESHED

A WARM SPRING BREEZE

CLEAN CUT

ACRES OF GREEN

FAWN-LIKE INNOCENCE

ON THE DAY OF IT'S BIRTH

WITNESS THE MAJESTICS

OF YOU BEING MY FIRST

EXPRESSING HOW TOUCHED I WAS WITH MY GIFT, I

ENCOURAGE HIM TO TAKE ME THROUGH THE STEPS ON

HOW HE CREATED IT. UNLIKE THE ONE HE DID FOR ME, IT

USUALLY TAKES HIM MORE THAN A WEEK TO DO.

LEADING ME INTO HIS OFFICE/WALK-IN CLOSET,

THINKING IT WOULD BE UNFAIR HE OPTS JUST TO

EXPLAIN THE ONE HE'S CURRENTLY WORKING ON FOR

THE AFRICAN ART EXPO.

THINKING I WAS MISSING SOMETHING, I ASK,

"WHAT'S THE ONE YOU MADE FOR ME CALLED? WHAT'S

IT'S TITLE?"

HE SMILES. "MFL."

CONFUSED, I ASK "MFL?"

"YEAH," HE SAYS. "MY FIRST LOVE."

FURFILLING HIS WORD, IN THE EARLY AFTERNOON,

HE TOOK ME SHOPPING AT THE MAJOR SHOPPING CENTER

AT 9TH AND MARKET STREETS. BY FOUR PM, AFTER THREE

AND A HALF HOURS OF SHOPPING, I HAD ACCUMULATED

THREE PAIR OF JEANS, A PAIR OF SNEAKERS, ONE OF

HEELS, AND TWO LOGO'D T-SHIRT. AS WE ATE IN THE

FOOD COURT, I ASKED HIM WHAT HE THINKS WOULD GO

GOOD WITH THE NEW PAIR OF HEELS FOR MY INTERVIEW.

HE SMILED AT ME. "CAN YOU DANCE IN HEELS?"

"IS THE SKY BLUE? I'M A DANCER, I CAN DANCE IN ANYTHING."

"HIS EYEBROWS RAISE AS A SMILE SLOWLY CREEPS ACROSS HIS FACE.

"SERIOUSLY CHRIS?" I SAY BASHFULLY, LOOKING AROUND AT THE OTHER PATRONS, TO SEE IF THEY CAUGHT HIS SEXUAL MEANING.

"I ONLY ASKED BECAUSE SINCE YOU ARE A DANCER, THEN DANCE FOR THEM IN WHATEVER YOU'RE MOST COMFORTABLE IN. THEN, EXPLAIN WHAT DANCE MEANS TO YOU AND WHY IT IS SO IMPORTANT IN YOUR LIFE. WITH THE COMBINATION OF THE TWO, THE REST OF THE PHILADELPHIA SCHOOL DISTRICT WILL SEE THE SAME THING MR. COMBS AND I BOTH SEE, A STAR.

CHAPTER 11

MORE

I FINALLY DID MAKE IT AROUND TO CALLING SALEEM BACK OVER THE TWO WEEKS I STAYED WITH CHRIS. HE WAS FREAKING OUT BECAUSE TOYA WAS PREGNANT AND DIDN'T KNOW WHAT TO DO. CLAIMING BEING HELD UP IN THE HOUSE, WAITING FOR ME TO COME HOME. KUE DEMANDED HE NEEDED TO NOT BE THERE. EVEN THOUGH OUR FATHER IS BETTER THAN HE WAS ALL OF THREE WEEKS AGO, KUE BELIEVED IT BEST THAT IF SOMEONE DID HAVE TO STAY AND AID OUR FATHERS BETTERMENT THAT IT BE SOMEONE OTHER THAN SALEEM WHO STILL HOLDS A GRUDGE AGAINST HIM. AND JUST COMING HOME FROM PRISON, KUE, YES, HE LOVES HIS FATHER, BUT FELT, AGAIN, RESTRICTED IN HIS MOVEMENTS AS HE BECAME OUR FATHERS SOLE CAREGIVER.

BASKING IN THE QUIETNESS ON MY RIDE HOME, I THINK OF ALL THE NEW THINGS I TRIED AND DID THAT CHRIS HAD INTRODUCED ME TO. HE ALLOWED ME TO TRY

MORE

MY HAND AT PAINTING. I WASN'T TO GOOD AT IT HONESTLY, BUT JUST TO HAVE THE EXPERIENCE TO SHARE IN WHAT HE LOVES GAVE ME JOY. HE TAUGHT ME HOW TO PLAY TENNIS, WHICH IN A WAY I ACTUALLY ENJOYED. IT DEFINITELY BEATS GOING TO THE GYM, AS YOU'RE CERTAIN TO GET A WORKOUT. BUT MY ALL TIME TASTE BUD FAVORITE WAS LAMB. SUCH A CONTRAST TO COME FROM A LIFE WITH NEW EXPERIENCES, BACK TO THE ONE I CAME FROM; A LIFE WHERE I MIGHT NEVER HAVE KNOWN THEM.

"THIS IS A SLAP IN THE FACE FROM REALITY."

"HOW SO?" HE ASKS, PARKING A FEW DOORS DOWN FROM MY OWN.

I GESTURE FOR HIM TO TAKE A LOOK AROUND.

"IF YOU ARE NOT HAPPY YANI, ONLY YOU HAVE THE POWER TO CHANGE IT. THE TIME YOU SPENT WITH ME, WERE YOU HAPPY? WASN'T THAT A REALITY?"

MORE

"YES," I TAKE A LOOK IN THE SIDE PASSENGER MIRROR. "MY FAMILY."

"IT WOULD BE SELFISH OF ME TO ASK YOU TO CHOOSE BETWEEN ME OR YOUR FAMILY. WHAT I AM ASKING IS, WHAT *YOU* THINK IS BEST FOR YOU?"

"I NEVER THOUGHT ABOUT IT LIKE THAT. IT ALWAYS FELT LIKE IT WAS US AGAINST THE WORLD; THAT IT WAS OUR JOB TO BE THERE FOR ONE ANOTHER."

"AND NOW?" CHRIS ASKS.

"I DON 'T KNOW."

WE SHARE A KISS BEFORE I GET OUT OF THE CAR. OPENING THE FRONT DOOR, I TURN BACK, JUST AS HE BEGINS DRIVING OFF. I HAD HALF A MIND TO RUN AFTER HIM AT THE SIGHT OF DISARRAY. MAKING IT TO MY ROOM, I TRY NOT TO TRIP OVER ANYTHING AND REVEL IN THE FACT, AT LEAST IT BEING JUST AS I LEFT IT. IMMEDIATELY, I BEGIN PRACTICING MY ROUTINE I PUT TOGETHER FOR MY MEETING WITH THE BOARD

MORE

MEMBERS. I STILL DON'T KNOW WHAT IT IS I'M GOING TO WEAR, LET ALONE, WHAT I AM GOING TO SAY. THESE DANCE MOVES THOUGH WILL HAVE A BLIND MAN GIVING ME A STANDING OVATION.

SALEEM WALKS IN AND LIES ACROSS MY BED, WATCHING ME PRACTICE.

"WHAT?" I ASK, NOT MESSING A BEAT.

"HAVEN'T SEEN YOU DANCE IN A WHILE, THAT'S ALL. HOME BOY MUST BE DOING SOMETHING RIGHT."

"NONE OF YOUR BUSINESS," I SING.

"YOU SEEM LIKE YOU'RE HAPPY."

"I AM, ARE YOU?"

"I'M AIGHT."

I STOP DANCING AND TURN OFF THE CONTEMPORARY MUSIC. "THEN WHY ARE YOU RUNNING AWAY FROM YOUR RESPONSIBILITY?"

"YOU TRIPPIN', I AIN'T RUNNING. I AIN'T SCARED OF NOTHING."

"THEN WHY ARE YOU HERE, INSTEAD OF HELPING TOYA GET READY?"

"I DON'T THINK I'M READY." MY QUESTIONING STARE GETS HIM TO CONTINUE, "I AIN'T TRYNA TREAT MY YOUNGIN LIKE CHUCK TREATED US."

MY CELL PHONE BEGINS TO RING AND I TELL SALEEM, "LET ME PUT YOU DOWN WITH A SECRET, YOU READY?"

"WHAT IS IT?"

"YOU ALREADY KNOW WHAT A BAD FATHER LOOKS AND ACTS LIKE, SO ALL YOU HAVE TO DO IS BE A TOTAL OPPOSITE OF HOW CHUCK IS AND YOU'LL BE A GREAT FATHER, TRUST ME, YOU'RE ALREADY ON THE RIGHT PATH. ALL YOU HAVE TO DO IS KEEP IT UP."

MORE

SEEING WHAT KUE WANTED, I ANSWER MY PHONE AND WE GO BACK AND FORTH OVER HIM ASKING ME, "IS EVERYTHING IN ORDER?" I LOVE MY BROTHER DEARLY, BUT FELT HURT AT THE THOUGHT OF HIS ONLY REASON FOR WANTING ME TO COME HOME, WAS TO CLEAN? FORTUNATELY, MOST OF THE THINGS LYING AROUND WAS SALEEM'S AND AFTER HEARING MY SIDE OF THE CONVERSATION, HE HELPED ME STRAIGHTEN UP, COMMENTING OF HOW HE THOUGHT CHRIS WAS A GOOD DUDE AND GIVING ME HIS APPROVAL.

FOLLOWED BY KENDLE AND C-NOTE, KUE WALKS IN WITH BAGS OF CHINESE FOOD, SPEAKING ONLY TO KENDLE AS I GO THROUGH THE BAGS, SHE JOINS ME UP THE STAIRS, AS SALEEM BURSTS INTO LAUGHTER. IN MY ROOM, CHATTING IT UP AND EATING, WITHIN TEN MINUTES, KENDLE'S PHONE RINGS. SHE EXPLAINS THAT THERE IS NOTHING WRONG WITH ME AND IMMEDIATELY, I KNEW SHE WAS TALKING TO KUE.

MORE

"THINGS STARTING TO GET SERIOUS BETWEEN YOU TWO, HUNH?" I ASK AS SOON AS SHE HANGS UP.

"SOMETHING LIKE THAT, BUT NOT AS SERIOUS AS YOU AND CHRIS. I MEAN WE BOTH HAVE BEEN KNOWN TO SPEND *A NIGHT* WITH A DUDE, *BUT TWO WEEKS*?"

"I KNOW, BUT HE'S JUST SO DIFFERENT THAN ALL THE DUDES I TALKED TO. AND, THE CRAZY THING IS, IT DIDN'T EVEN SEEM LIKE TWO WEEKS WHEN I WAS WITH HIM."

"YA'LL TWO MUST BE HAVING ONE HELL OVA TIME," SHE COMMENTS.

"LIKE YOU WOULDN'T BELIEVE."

I PERFORM MY ROUTINE FOR HER AND WHEN I FINISHED, I ASKED MY NOSY GUEST WHAT THEY THOUGHT.

"YOU COULD HAVE DONE THAT DOWNSTAIRS."

"AND WHY WOULD I DO THAT?"

MORE

KUE ANSWERS, "ENTERTAINMENT." AND I FLIP. WE ARGUE ABOUT ME NOT BEING A STRIPPER. I TELL HIM THAT I AM NOT HERE TO BE NO ONES "ENTERTAINMENT" AND OF HIM BELITTLING ME. TEARS FLOWING FROM MY EYES, HE DIDN'T TRY TO STOP ME AS I PUSHED PAST HIM TOWARDS THE STEPS. I THINK THAT HURT EVEN MORE.

"I WOULDN'T GET IN THE MIDDLE OF THAT HOME BOY," I HEAR SALEEM SAY AS I WALK OUT OF THE FRONT DOOR.

NOT CARING WHOSE FOOTSTEPS AND VOICE WAS CALLING ME, I KEPT ON WALKING. UNDER THE BRIDGE, THE PERSON HAD CAUGHT UP WITH ME, GRABBED MY ARM AND WITH A WILD SWING, I TURNED AROUND YET MY PUNCH WAS CAUGHT IN MID AIR.

"NICE SWING, FOR A GIRL," C-NOTE ADMITS.

"LEAVE ME ALONE." I TRY TO WALK AWAY, BUT COULDN'T LOOSEN FROM HIS GRIP.

MORE

"WHAT, YOU DON'T GOT NO RAP FOR ME? I WAS JUST TRYNA SEE IF YOU WERE AIGHT."

"WHAT, YOU BLIND? CAN 'T YOU SEE I'M NOT. NOW LET ME GO." I PULL AWAY FROM HIM.

CRUSHING ME INTO A RECESSED MAINTENANCE DOORWAY, FOR THE TRAIN TRACKS ABOVE, AMIDST THE COBBERSTONE WALL, C-NOTE PRESSES

HIS 5'10, 180 POUND BODY AGAINST MY 5'5, 130 TO WHERE I CAN'T MOVE. PROMISING ME HE WOULD END MY MISERABLE LIFE IF I SCREAMED NO MATTER HOW BEAUTIFUL I AM. WITH A GUN AS EVIDENCE IN MY FACE, I DID NOT CRY WHILE CONTEMPLATING DYING. I DID BEGIN CRYING WHEN HE ACTED ON HIS FANTASY TO SEE IF I WAS AS GOOD AS CHRIS SAID I WAS. NOTHING AT ALL LIKE CHRIS, C-NOTE DRYLY RAMMED HIMSELF INSIDE MY BEHIND, HARD AND FAST.

BEING RAPED ISN'T SUPPOSED TO BE FUN, OR AT ALL CONSIDERATE BUT I

MORE

THOUGHT OF ASKING HIM TO USE MY TEARS AS LUBRICATION, BUT DIDN'T WANT TO MAKE THE SITUATION WORSE ON MYSELF. AND BESIDES, AFTER HE FINISHES GETTING WHAT HE WANTED, I'LL NEVER SEE HIM AGAIN. OR SO I THOUGHT.

RECOCKING THE GUN, AFTER WIPING THE BACKSPLASH ON HIS PRIVATE AREA ON MY SHIRT, HE SAYS, "RULE 1: WE DO NOT SPEAK OF THIS, WHAT HAPPENED TONIGHT, TO ANYONE, CAPRICE? IF YOU DO, YOU AND WHOMEVER YOU TOLD WILL BE SIX FEET UNDER. RULE 2: YOU GOT TWENTY FOUR HOURS TO BREAK UP WITH CHRIS, OR I WILL MAKE YOU WATCH, AS I KILL HIM, THEN I'LL KILL YOU. YOU <u>MY</u> GIRL NOW"

PULLING MY HAIR TO THE SIDE, SMELLING IT, HE SAYS, "I DON'T SHARE."

CHAPTER 12

EYES HEAVY FROM WANTING TO GO TO SLEEP, BUT I KEEP THEM OPEN BECAUSE I DON'T WANT THE REOCCURING NIGHTMARE EVEN MORE. I JUMP AT THE SOUND OF FOOTSTEPS COMING UP THE STAIRS, SALEEM APPEARS IN MY DOORWAY AND I QUICKLY PULL MY COMFORTER UP OVER MY HEAD. MY CELL PHONE RINGS, I HEAR CLICKING, THEN THE POWER OFF TUNE.

HE SITS ON MY BED, "YOU GOT ME SCARED, YO." WHEN I DIDN'T INQUIRE WHY, HE GAVE IT. "AT FIRST, WHEN I CALLED YOU AND DIDN'T GET AN ANSWER, I THOUGHT YOU WAS AT WORK. THEN WHEN YOUR JOB CALLED ME AS YOUR EMERGENCY CONTACT, SAYING YOU DIDN'T SHOW UP, I KNEW SOMETHING WAS UP."

SILENCE.

"AND, THE ICING ON THE CAKE WAS WHEN I CAME OVER HERE, YOUR HOMEBOY, CHRIS WAS PARKED OUTSIDE, SAYING THAT HE HAD BEEN CALLING AND KNOCKING FOR THE PAST HOUR TO TAKE YOU TO SOME

MORE

DANCE INTERVIEW THAT," HE CHECKS HIS WATCH, "YOU MISSED NOW."

I TAKE A DEEP BREATH TO HELP HOLD BACK THE TEARS AT THE MENTION OF CHRIS' NAME AND THE MISSED OPPORTUNITY HE WENT OUT OF HIS WAY TO SET UP FOR ME. I FEEL LIKE SUCH A DISAPPOINTMENT.

"YANI," SALEEM PULLS ON MY COMFORTER, BUT I TIGHTEN MY GRIP. "IF YOU AIN'T GONNA TALK, AT LEAST LET ME CHECK YOU OUT, TO MAKE SURE YOU'RE AIGHT FOR MYSELF."

I ALLOW HIM TO UNCOVER ME, BUT ONLY DOWN TO MY WAIST REVEALING THAT I AM STILL WEARING THE SHIRT FROM YESTERDAY. AS IF I WERE A CHILD, LIKE HE SAID, HE STARTED CHECKING ME; FIRST, FOR OBVIOUS BRUISES OR MARKS. THEN, WITH THE BACK OF HIS HAND, FLUSH AGAINST MY FOREHEAD AND CHEEK, COMMENTING THAT I DID FEEL WARM.

MORE

WHEN ASKING WHAT I FELT LIKE DIDN'T RENDER A RESPONSE, HE BREAKS IT DOWN EVEN SIMPLER, "IS IT THAT TIME OF THE MONTH?" I ROLL MY EYES, INSIDE I WANTED TO SMILE.

ONLY SALEEM, "YOU FEEL LIKE THROWING UP?" I NOD AFTER GIVING IT SOME THOUGHT, BUT FIGURED NOTHING WOULD PROBABLY EVEN COME OUT AS I HAVEN'T EATEN IN NEARLY TWENTY FOUR HOURS. "MORNING SICKNESS?"

LORD, I HOPE NOT. I SHAKE MY HEAD NO.

"COME ON YANI, I'M TRYING, TALK TO ME. I AIN'T GOOO AT THIS KINDA STUFF LIKE YOU. DID SOMEONE DO SOMETHING TO YOU? HURT YOU?" HE PLEADS.

I LOOK AWAY AND TURN OVER.

"FUCK! MAN, SHIT!" HE GETS UP AND STARTS PACING. "WHO YANI? I SWEAR TO - MAN, JUST TELL ME WHO…,"

HEARING A FAINT SOUND, I PEEK OUT OF MY COVERS, AS SALEEM TURNS TO THE DOOR.

"HEY MAN, SHE AIN'T TALKIN'. SOMETHING HAPPENED TO HER. SOMEBODY DID SOMETHING." I HEAR A PAIR OF FEET SHUFFLE OUT, I LOOK BACK AND SEE CHRIS STANDING AT MY DOOR. MY TEARS BREAK THROUGH THEIR LEVEES LIKE KATRINA DID NEW ORLEANS. I COULDN'T EVEN FACE THE CLOSEST PERSON TO ME IN THE WORLD. HOW AM I SUPPOSED TO TELL THE ONLY PERSON WHO SHOWED ME THAT THERE'S MORE TO LIFE THAN WHAT I ALREADY KNOW. AND, ON TOP OF THAT, TELL HIM IN ORDER TO SAVE HIS LIFE, I HAVE TO END THE ONE HE INTRODUCED ME TO.

TAKING MY HAND, AS HE KNELT DOWN BESIDE MY BED, I SOB EVEN HARDER. WHEN I QUIET TO SNIFFLES, NO MORE TEARS REMAINING, HE SAYS, "I'M SURE KNOW YOU HAVE PEOPLE WHO CARE A GREAT DEAL ABOUT YOU, BUT YOU WILL HAVE TO BE *WILLING* TO ACCEPT THE HELP." LOOKING AT MY HAND AS HE RUBS IT, HE

CONTINUES, "HOWEVER MUCH I LOVE YOU, I FEEL …

HELPLESS."

A BRIEF MOMENT COMES TO WHERE HE DOESN'T

SAY ANYTHING. HE STANDS UP AND KISSES MY

FOREHEAD. WHEN HE STANDS, I SEE C-NOTE IN THE

DOORWAY.

"I'LL GIVE YOU YOUR SPACE," CHRIS TELLS ME AND

I WOULD GUESS BY HEARING WHAT HE NEEDED, C-NOTE

DISAPPEARS AS QUIETLY AS HE CAME. "AND, I WILL WAIT

FOR YOU TO RECOVER FROM WHATEVER … AILS YOU,"

HE SAYS, AS IF ON SOME LEVEL, HE KNEW.

FOR THE NEXT DAY AND A HALF, SALEEM WAS

CONSTANTLY CHECKING IN ON ME, SO MUCH SO, THAT AT

TIMES, RESORTED TO TAKING NAPS AT THE FOOT OF MY

BED. THE PAIN GETTING BETTER, PHYSICALLY, YET

CONCERNED ABOUT GETTING BED SORES, I DECIDE TO

TAKE A SHOWER. CARELESSLY, I DRESS IN SWEATS AS

SALEEM BRINGS ME A FRUIT SMOOTHIE AND GRILLED

CHICKEN SALAD WITH THE WORKS, CLAIMING TO CATCH ME UP ON ALL OF THE VITAMINS AND NUTRIENTS I MISSED OUT ON THE PAST COUPLE OF DAYS. I SMILE IN THE FACT OF HIS CONCERN, HIS OVER PROTECTIVENESS, HIS NEGLIGENCE OF HIMSELF AND THAT HE ACTUALLY LEARNED SOMETHING FROM MY NURSE TRAINING.

SOMETHING, THAT FOR HIM, I THOUGHT WAS LONG GONE. LEARNING NEW

THINGS, THAT IS. WHAT ENDED MY SMILE WAS WHEN HE MENTIONED THAT KUE ASKED HIM HOW I WAS. IT WAS THEN, DID I REALIZE THAT KUE, NOT ONCE, CAME TO CHECK ON ME HIMSELF THESE PAST THREE DAYS. SALEEM SUGGESTED THAT I CALL HIM, BUT I WASN'T FOR TALKING, LET ALONE TO HIM.

TAKING A GUESS AS TO WHY, HE EXPLAINS THAT KUE AND C-NOTE WENT TO ATLANTIC CITY FOR THE WEEKEND, WHICH FURTHER INFURIATED ME. NOT ONLY AT THE MERE MENTION OF THE PERSON'S NAME WHO

MORE

FORCED THEIR WILL UPON ME, AT THE THREAT OF MY LIFE AND THE ONES I LOVE IF I HAPPENED TO TELL, BUT HE AND KUE BEING JOINED AT THE HIP, THE INSURMOUNTABLE NOTION OF KUE HAVING AN INCLINATION OF WHAT HAPPENED AND DID NOTHING TO PREVENT IT. AND, ON TOP OF THAT, STILL HANGS OUT WITH HIM.

A LITTLE AFTER THE SUN HAD SET, WHILE SALEEM AND I WERE WATCHING A MOVIE, KUE AND C-NOTE WALK IN.

"LOOKS LIKE SOMEONE'S FEELING BETTER," KUE STATES MATTER OF FACTLY.

"IS EVERYTHING THAT GLITTERS, GOLD?" I PROMPT.

BUT IT WAS C-NOTE WHO ANSWERED AS HE PLOPPED DOWN NEXT TO ME, "WHY WOULDN'T IT BE?"

I CRINGE AND WITH A PUZZLING LOOK, AS HE'S THE ONLY ONE WHO NOTICES MY SUDDEN DISCOMFORT, I LOOK AWAY FROM SALEEM'S QUESTIONING GAZE.

THEY GO ON TO SHARE THEIR TALES OF THE TIME THEY SHARED IN THE EAST COASTS 'SIN CITY'. AFTERWARDS, C-NOTE RELAYS OF HOW HE GOT KUE A SESSION IN THE STUDIO TO LAY DOWN SOME TRACKS.

EXCITEDLY, KUE RESPONDS, "YO, THAT'S NOT SOMETHING TO BE PLAYING AROUND WITH LIKE THAT MAN; YOU KNOW HOW I FEEL 'BOUT MY BARS."

"I KNOW BRO-BRO, AND THAT'S WHY YOU GONNA OPEN UP THE SHOW FOR ME NEXT FRIDAY, WITH ME AND MY SHORTIE WATCHING FROM BACKSTAGE. AIN'T THAT RIGHT?"

I LOOK UP, AND EVERYBODY'S EYES ARE ON ME. LOST, IN MY OWN THOUGHTS, AIMLESSLY TWIDDLING MY THUMBS, I WASN'T EVEN PAYING ATTENTION, SO, I SIMPLY NOD MY HEAD.

MORE

KUE GETS TO HOOPING AND HOLLERING, SO I KNOW I MUST HAVE GIVEN THE RIGHT RESPONSE AS HE SHAKES C-NOTE'S HAND, THEY HUG.

LED OUT OF THE HOUSE BY SALEEM, WE HEAD TO THE CHINESE STORE FOR FOOD THAT THEY ORDERED. THE WALK TO AND THE BRIEF WAIT WAS QUIET, BUT I FELT THE UNDERLYING REASON TO WHY HE ASKED ME TO WALK WITH HIM. HITTING THE CONCRETE AGAIN, HE BROKE OUR SILENCE.

"I'M FAR FROM THE SMARTEST DUDE AROUND, AI.GHT, BUT I KNOW THAT *I*, KNOW *YOU*, JUST AS GOOD AS YOU KNOW ME. SO, HELP ME WITH SOMETHINGS. YOU CAN DO THAT, RIGHT?"

I NOD IN ACKNOWLEDGMENT.

"WHY YOU LEAVE CHRIS FOR DUDE? I THOUGHT YOU WAS HAPPY WITH HIM."

"I WAS."

"THEN, WHY?"

I SHAKE MY HEAD NO, TO WHICH HE SIGHS.

"IS HE 'BETTER' THAN CHRIS?"

AGAIN, I SHAKE MY HEAD NO.

''ALRIGHT, WE ON THE SAME PAGE AT LEAST."

HE STOPS WALKING AND OUT OF FEAR OF MY INABILITY TO WITHHOLD THE TRUTH FROM HIM ANY LONGER, ESPECIALLY IF HE ASKS THE RIGHT QUESTIONS, WITH A DOWN CAST FACE, I TURN TO HIM. "LET IT GO."

"NAW, I CAN'T. I—"

"PLEASE, SALEEM. LEAVE IT ALONE."

"BUT,"

WITH TEARS FALLING, I LIFT MY FACE AND FOCUS MY EYES ON HIS. HIS OBJECTION FADES AS HE EMBRACES ME. HE APOLOGIZES A FEW TIMES AND EXPLAINS I HAVE NOTHING TO CRY OVER. HE DIDN'T MEAN TO PUSH ME, HE

MORE

SEES THAT I AM NOT READY TO TALK ABOUT IT, THAT THINGS JUST WASN'T ADDING UP TO HIM AND HE WAS TRYING TO FIGURE OUT WHY.

WE GET TO THE WALKWAY LEADING TO OUR HOUSE AND HE STOPS ME.

"ONE QUESTION AND I PROMISE IT WILL BE THE LAST ONE I ASK. THIS IS IMPORTANT. DEPENDING ON HOW YOU ANSWER, I'LL KNOW WHAT TO DO, FAIR ENOUGH?"

"YEAH."

HE ASKS, "WERE YOU <u>ASKING</u> ME, OR <u>TELLING</u> ME TO LEAVE THE SITUATION ALONE?"

I SMILE. IT NEVER CEASES TO AMAZE ME OF HOW MY BROTHERS MIND WORKS. LIKE I ALWAYS SAID, MY BROTHERS MAY NOT BE THE SHARPEST KNIVES IN THE DRAWER, BUT **HOT DAMN** IF THEY GET STRAIGHT TO THE POINT. KNOWING WHERE HE WAS GETTING AT, I TELL HIM, WITH ABSOLUTE CERTAINTY THAT I WAS "TELLING HIM" TO LEAVE IT ALONE.

MORE

IF WE WEREN'T FOURTEEN MONTHS APART, ONE WOULD THINK WE ARE TWINS. THINKING FOR A MOMENT, HIS FACE THEN MIRRORED MINE AND WE ENTERED THE HOUSE.

CHAPTER 13

I WAS TOLD I WAS FIRED FROM MY JOB FOR M.I.A (BEING MISSING IN ACTION) AND C-NOTE COULDN'T HAVE CARED LESS, STATING, "HIS" WOMAN DIDN'T NEED TO WORK ANYWAY. NOR, DID HE WANT ME TO. BEFORE COMPLYING WITH HIS NEXT DEMAND, I SET UP DIRECT DEPOSIT FOR MY UNEMPLOYMENT CHECKS OVER THE PHONE WHILE MY THINGS WERE BEING LOADED INTO SALEEM'S CAR. MOVING TO C-NOTE'S MOTHER'S BASEMENT, JUST OFF 66TH AND OGONTZ, IS SUCH A CONTRAST FROM CHRIS, THAT I INTERNALLY LAUGH AT THIS 29-YEAR-OLD HIGH SCHOOL DROP OUT, HARDCORE

RAPPER WANT-TO-BE; SO UNREALISTIC. I'M GLAD I DIDN'T TELL ANYONE THAT I HAD MONEY IN THE BANK. EVERYTHING HE OWNS ... SEEMS DINGY.

THE FIRST NIGHT, I PRAYED THAT IT WOULDN'T HAPPEN AGAIN, BUT IN THE BACK OF MY MIND, I EXPECTED IT TO. AGAIN, HE FORCED ME TO HAVE SEX, WHICH TURNED INTO ME BEING A PUNCHING BAG. NOT AGREEING WITH A MAN EVER PUTTING HIS HANDS ON A WOMAN, HIS ROOT OF HIS ANGER DID HAVE SOME SEMBLANCE OF MERIT. I WAS JUST LYING THERE, MIND WANDERING. SHOOT, I DEFINITELY DIDN'T ENJOY MYSELF, SO I GUESS WE BOTH HAD CAUSE TO BE UPSET.

OR, COULD THE REAL REASON OF HIM BEING UPSET, WAS OF ME NOT GIVING IT TO HIM THE WAY HE WANTED SO THAT HE COULD ENJOY HIMSELF? TO BE HONEST, I DIDN'T WANT TO GIVE HIM ANYTHING, IN THE FIRST PLACE. HE TOOK IT. AND IF HE WANTED SOMETHING THAT DESPERATELY, WHY SHOULD I, HAVE TO HELP?

NOT WANTING TO GET BEAT ANYMORE, I BEGAN TO FAKE IT; ESPECIALLY SINCE THERE WASN'T ANYONE TO SAVE ME IN THIS MUSKY, DINGY BASEMENT APARTMENT. TO SAVE MYSELF FROM FUTURE BEATINGS, I BEGIN FAKING MY FEELINGS FOR HIM, HIS LACK OF STYLE AND FINESSE. IF HE WASN'T APART OF THE ITTY-BITTY-DICKY COMMITTEE, HIS LACK OF SEX GAME PROBABLY WOULDN'T BE A PROBLEM.

THE RARE OCCASSIONS I DID GET BEAT, WAS WHEN I WASN'T READY FOR ONE OF HIS SHOWS HE WANTED ME TO ATTEND SO THAT HE COULD SHOW ME OFF. WEARING SOMETHING TO TIGHT AND/OR REVEALING TO ONE OF HIS SHOWS. HIS FOOD NOT BEING COOKED BY THE TIME HE GOT HOME. OR COLD BY THE TIME HE GOT THERE SINCE HIS ARRIVAL TIMES WAS ALWAYS SPORADIC. THE ONE AND ONLY TIME HE EVER APOLOGIZED FOR BEATING ME WAS WHEN HE CAME HOME EXPECTING FRIED CHICKEN AND I HAD COOKED A TUNA CASSEROLE. HE APOLOGIZED

SIMPLY BECAUSE HE DIDN'T BRING ANY CHICKEN FROM HIS MOTHER'S FREEZER FOR ME TO FRY.

I COULDN'T HAVE TOLD YOU THE DATE I WAS FINALLY ABLE TO SEE AND SPEND TIME WITH MY FAMILY IF IT WEREN'T FOR THE MANY BUS DETOURS CAUSE BY BLOCK PARTIES AND COOK OUTS. THE 4TH OF JULY. MY FATHER HAD JUST LEFT HIS IN-PATIENT PROGRAM JUST THE DAY BEFORE CLAIMING THAT THEY COULDN'T TELL HIM ANYTHING THAT HE DIDN'T ALREADY KNOW. I FELT OUT OF TOUCH WITH KENDLE AND TOYA; BY MY LONESOME, AS I WAS ALWAYS UNDER THE WATCHFUL EYE OF C-NOTE.

IT WASN'T LONG BEFORE SALEEM JOINS ME, WHICH INCREASES C-NOTE'S ATTENTION. IF I DIDN'T KNOW ANY BETTER, I'D SAY HE WAS TRYING TO READ MY LIPS.

"SOMEBODY BEEN BUSY," SALEEM STATES.

"NOT REALLY."

MORE

"YOU AIN'T BEEN AROUND TOO MUCH. WHAT'S THAT ABOUT?"

I GAZE INTO MY CLASPED HANDS ATOP MY SKIRT, UNRESPONSIVE.

"UN-HUNH." HE GOES ON TELLING ME OF HOW, THANKS TO MY ADVICE HE AND TOYA HAS BEEN GOING STEADY. NO ARGUMENTS OR FIGHTS. AND ON TOP OF THAT, THEY FOUND OUT THAT THEY WERE HAVING A BABY GIRL.

I CONGRATULATE HIM AND ASK IF THEY HAD THOUGHT OF ANY NAMES. SALEEM DENIES CLAIMING THAT THEY THOUGHT IT WAS TOO EARLY. ALTHOUGH TOYA HAS STARTED RECEIVING W.I.C. (FOOD FOR WOMEN, INFANTS AND CHILDREN) AND SUPPOSE TO BE GETTING A NEW PLACE FROM THIS PROGRAM FOR FIRST TIME MOMS. THE PROGRAM ALSO HAVE ALREADY STARTED

MORE

SUPPLYING THEM WITH A CRIB, NEWBORN CLOTHS, DIAPERS AND EVEN MATERNITY CLOTHES FOR TOYA.

"SEEMS LIKE I MISSED ALOT, HUNH?" I ASK.

BEFORE SALEEM GETS A CHANCE TO ANSWER, SHOUTS BREAK OUT. NOT TOO SOON AFTER, YOU HEAR SOMEONES FACE GETTING IMPACTED BY ANOTHER FIST. AS ALWAYS, WHAT HAPPENS WHEN A FIGHT BREAKS OUT? CONVERSATIONS STOPS AS EVERYONES' ATTENTION FOCUSES ON THE FIGHT. SOMETHING I WASN'T PREPARED FOR OR EXPECTED TO SEE WAS IT BEING BETWEEN KUE AND C-NOTE.

IT WAS KUE'S VOICE WHO WAS THE ONE SHOUTING AT FIRST, UNTIL HE WAS HIT. HE WAS SHOUTING SOMETHING ABOUT NOT RECEIVING HIS FULL END OF THE DEAL, TOO BAD FOR C-NOTE. THAT WAS THE ONLY HIT HE GOT OFF. THE WORST DECISION HE COULD HAVE MADE. NO ONE BUT SALEEM WAS BRAVE ENOUGH TO PULL KUE UP OFF C-NOTE BEFORE KUE PUMMELLED HIM

TO DEATH. SURE, I COULD HAVE, BUT I WAS ENJOYING SEEING C-NOTE GET THE CRAP BEAT OUT OF HIM FOR A CHANGE.

GIVING HIM SPACE TO RECOVER, AND MAKE A SILENT ESCAPE, PEOPLE TURNED TO THOSE NEAREST AND CARRIED ON WITH THEIR PRIOR CONVERSATIONS.

STANDING IN FRONT OF ME WITH A LOOK I DON'T QUITE UNDERSTAND C-NOTE GETS TOLD BY KUE, "GET THE FUCK OUTTA HERE, HOMES, SHE AIN'T GOIN' NOWHERE WITH YOU."

"IF SHE KNOWS WHATS GOOD FOR YOU, SHE WILL." C-NOTE SPITS OUT BLOOD AND LEAVES.

I TRY TO FOLLOW, UNNOTICED BY KUE, AS HE'S ARGUING WITH SALEEM FOR HOLDING HIM BACK FROM GOING AFTER C-NOTE AGAIN, BUT MY ATTEMPT FAILED. I QUICKEN MY STEP, FIRST, TO GET AWAY FROM THE SLURS THROWN MY WAY BY THE ONE WHO HAS TAKEN

MORE

CARE OF ME, MOST OF MY LIFE. SECONDLY, TO CATCH UP TO THE SCUMBAG LOSER KUE SAYS I'M FOLLOWING.

CHAPTER 14

NOT KNOWING WHAT'S ON THE HORIZON HAS GOTTEN ME WORRIED, ANXIOUS AND A LITTLE SCARED OUT OF MY MIND. IT'S BEEN A LITTLE OVER A WEEK NOW AND C-NOTE HASN'T TOUCHED NOR SPOKEN TO ME. IT'S NOT THE FACT THAT I WANT HIM TO, BUT IT'S NOT LIKE HIM NOT TO DO SO EITHER. HE'S BEEN MUMBLING TO HIMSELF. THE BITS AND PIECES I CATCH ARE USUALLY CURSES TO HIMSELF. HE EVEN LOOKS AT ME DIFFERENTLY NOW. A FARAWAY LOOK THAT I KNOW CAN'T BE GOOD.

SO BADLY, DO I WANT TO REACH OUT TO MY BROTHERS AND EXPLAIN WHY I LEFT, OF C-NOTE'S UNPREDICTABILITY AND PROMISE OF ENDING MY LIFE AS

MORE

WELL AS WHOSE EVER I SIDE WITHAGAINST HIM. WOULD THEY UNDERSTAND MY REASONING? WHY I CAME TO THE CONCLUSION I DID? WOULD THEY HAVE MADE THE SAME DECISION THAT I HAVE? SHOULD I HAVE TOLD THEM WHY AND WHAT'S BEEN GOING ON SOONER?

MY ANXIETY DEEPENS WHEN, AFTER NOT COMING HOME FOR A FEW DAYS C-NOTE TAKES ME OUT. SOMETHING HE'S NEVER DONE BEFORE. HE SET UP A NICE PICNIC IN FAIRMOUNT PARK ALONG THE SCHYLLKILL RIVER, OPPOSITE OF BOATHOUSE ROW. IT WAS BEAUTIFUL, CONSIDERING. THE SUN SHONE BRIGHTLY AND WITH THE OCCASIONAL BREEZE, THE 85 DEGREE WEATHER'S HUMIDITY TOLERABLE.

HE BEGAN TO OPEN UP TO ME ABOUT HIS LIFE, PAST RELATIONSHIPSAND HOW HE ENDED UP IN THE RAP INDUSTRY. THE CONVERSATION STEERED TO HOW HE ENDED UP STILL LIVING AT HOME WITH HIS MOTHER. HE JUST FELT THE NEED TO ALWAYS BE THERE FCJL HER AND PROTECT HER. RIGHT, GO FIGURE. WITH THE WAY HE

MORE

PROTECTED HIMSELF AT THE COOKOUT, I HARDLY SEE HOW HE CAN PROTECT ANYBODY.

ACTUALLY, HE CONTINUES, THAT FEELING OF PROTECTING HIS MOTHER FIRST AROSE WHEN C-NOTE WAS TWELVE YEARS OLD AFTER WITNESSING THE MAN WHO RAISED HIM ABUSE HIS MOTHER, HE FINALLY GOT TIRED OF IT ONE DAY AND STOOD UP TO HIM, ONLY TO RECEIVE THE SAME. IT WAS THEN, EVELYN, C-NOTE'S MOTHER, TOOK HIM AND RAN TO AN ABUSE SHELTER FOR WOMEN AND CHILDREN. SHE EXPLAINED TO HIM, THAT SHE ONLY STAYED WITH HIM FOR SO LONG, BECAUSE SHE BELIEVED THAT A BOY SHOULD HAVE A MALE ROLE MODEL IN HIS LIFE, TO TEACH HIM HOW TO BE A MAN. BUT, ONCE HE DISPLAYED HIS ABUSE WAYS ON HIM, ONLY THEN DID SHE REALIZE THAT IT WAS TIME TO MOVE ON AND THAT HE JUST MIGHT NOT BE THE RIGHT MAN AS A ROLE MODEL FOR HER SON.

"I WAS DOING A LOT OF THINKING WHILE I WAS GONE. AFTER A CONVERSATION WITH MY MOTHER," HE

EXPLAINS, "SHE TOLD ME I WAS DOING THE SAME THINGS TO YOU MY "FATHER," FOR LACK OF A BETTER TERM, WAS DOING TO HER."

HE LOOKED LIKE HE WANTED TO KEEP ON TALKING BUT WAS TRYING TO FIND THE RIGHT WORDS, SO I KEPT QUIET. I DIDN'T KNOW WHAT TO SAY TO BEGIN WITH.

"I NEVER LOOKED AT IT THAT WAY. I KNOW I HURT YOU AND FOR THAT, I'M, SORRY. I DO CARE ABOUT YOU AND YOU PROBABLY DON'T EVEN BELIEVE ME. HUMPH, I HAVEN'T GIVEN YOU A REASON TO BELIEVE ME. BUT I DO CARE ABOUT YOU. YOU'RE MY GIRL AND I'M GONNA MAKE IT UP TO YOU.FIRST," HE SCRATCHES HIS HEAD. "I'M GOING TO DO SOMETHING YOU ARE NOT GOING TO LIKE. IT MIGHT HURT YOU, BUT IT HAS NOTHING TO DO WITH YOU, IT'S JUST SOMETHING I HAVE TAKE CARE OF. I ONLY HOPE YOU'LL FORGIVE ME."

I GET LEFT WITH MY THOUGHTS WHEN HE GETS UP AND WALKS DOWN A PATHWAY. MY EYES FOLLOW HIM

AS I WONDER IF THAT IS THE SAME GUY I HAVE BEEN LIVING WITH FOR THE PAST TWO MONTHS. OR, IF ANYTHING HE JUST TOLD ME HAD AN OUNCE OF TRUTH TO IT. AFTER HE DISAPPEARS AROUND A BEND, MY GAZE SWITCHES TO THE ROWERS, BOATING THE RIVER.

A SHORT TIME PAST BEFORE SOMEONE FLATLY STATED, "WHAT'S UP?"

DUSTING MYSELF OFF AS I STAND, I ASK KUERON, "HOW YOU BEEN?"

IN RESPONSE, HE SAYS, "YOU KNOW ME, I'M ALWAYS GOOD."

"SALEEM?"

"HIM TOO. YOU WOULD KNOW, IF YOU WERE WHERE YOU WERE SUPPOSED TO BE."

AGAIN, AT HIS STATEMENT, I'M AT A LOSS. NOT KNOWING WHAT TO DO.

HE CHECKS HIS WATCH. "YO MAN, TIME IS MONEY. YOU ALREADY MADE YOUR DECISION, SO WHY ARE YOU SENDING OUT A.P.B.'S TO MEET OUT HERE?"

"WHAT? I NEVER SENT YOU NO MESSAGES?"

"AIGHT, I'M OUT."

AS HE TURNS AROUND, A HOODED MAN APPROACHES, JUST CROSSED THE STREET, A METALLIC OBJECT AIMED DIRECTLY AT KUE'S FOREHEAD. WITHOUT TIME TO REACT, I HEARD A MUFFLED POP. THE EVENT DOESN'T REGISTER IN MY MIND. NOT EVEN WHEN THE RED LIQUID AND PINKISH GRAY MATTER SPRAYS OUT THE BACK OF KUE'S HEAD ONTO ME.

A PASSERBY SCREAMS. KUE'S BODY SLUMPS TO THE GROUND AND C-NOTE'S EYES MEETS MINE AS HE MOUTHS THE WORDS "I'M SORRY."

CHAPTER 15

MY LEGS RAN AS HARD AND FAST AS THEY COULD. WITHOUT A CONSCIOUS THOUGHT AS TO WHERE I ENDED UP, I ENTER THE STONE AND CONCRETE WALLED BACK YARD. THE HOUSE WAS SILENT WHEN I ENTERED, SO I WAITED. DARKNESS HAD LONG SINCE FELL BEFORE THE HOUSES OWNER RETURNED. STOPPED IN HIS TRACKS IN THE DOORWAY OF THE KITCHEN, HE FLICKS THE LIGHT SWITCH ILLUMINATING THE ROOM.

AS MY EYES ADJUST TO THE LIGHT, HE SITS ACROSS FROM ME AT THE KITCHEN TABLE. PICKING THE KEY UP OFF THE TABLE, HE SLOWLY TURNS IT BETWEEN HIS FINGERS. "PLACING THIS SPARE KEY BETWEEN THE HINGES OF THE GATE MUST'VE BEEN A GOOD IDEA. A BETTER ONE, IF YOU USED IT." HE PLACES IT BACK ON THE TABLE. NOTING THE OBVIOUS, HE STATES, "THERE'S SOMETHING ON YOUR MIND."

I NOD.

"WHENEVER YOU'RE READY," CHRIS SAYS.

MORE

I DON'T KNOW WHY IT HAPPENED, BUT FRANKLY, I DIDN'T CARE. THE HORRIFIC EVENTS FLOWED FREELY FROM MY LIPS AS HE LISTENED INTENSELY. FEELING FREED, AFTER FINALLY LETTING IT ALL OUT, I ANXIOUSLY AWAIT FOR HIM TO SAY SOMETHING, ANYTHING BESIDES THE RHYTHMIC TAP OF HIS FINGERS ATOP THE KITCHEN TABLE.

MY EXPECTATIONS OF A RESPONSE GETS DENIED AS HE ATTEMPTS TO REACH FOR MY HAND, I JUMP. NOT TAKING OFFENSE, HE OFFERS HIS ROOM AS HE TAKES HIS GUEST BED. MY ATTEMPTS AT SLEEP WAS WAY OFF BASE, AS I JUST LAID THERE, RESTING WHICH SEEMED TO BE ALL I REALLY NEEDED ANYWAY.

BY DAWN, I WANDERED TO HIS GUEST ROOM TO FIND HIM STARING AT A BLANK CANVAS. I CLEAR MY THROAT AND HE TURNS LOOKING AS RESTLESS AS I FEEL. HE ASKS ME IF I'M HUNGRY, I TEEL HIM I'M NOT.

MORE

"I NEED TO SEE YOUR BROTHER SALEEM," CHRIS TELLS ME.

MY EYES WIDEN IN THE THOUGHT OF HIM ATTAINING THE SAME FATE AS KUE. I RUSH BACK TO THE MASTER BEDROOM AND PICK UP THE PHONE. AT THE SOUND OF HIS SLEEPY VOICE, I BECAME OVERWHELMED WITH TEARS HEARING MY SOBS BEFORE I DROPPED THE CORDLESS; SALEEM BECOMES ALERT, FRANTICALLY ASKING, "WHAT'S GOING ON? WHAT HAPPENED?" IN A PLEADING, BUT DEMANDING TONE.

NOT BEING ABLE TO ACCEPT CHRIS WORD, CHRIS GETS SALEEM TO MEET US AT A DINER OUT ON THE BOULEVARD.

AT THE SIGHT OF ME STEPPING OUT OF THE CAR, SALEEM FLICKS HIS CIGARETTE. RUSHING TOWARDS US, HE SCREAMS, "WHAT THE FUCK HAPPENED?"

MORE

MY SOMBER FACE PROMPTS HIM TO EMBRACE ME IN HIS LINKY ARMS. HE ASKS CHRIS, "COME ON MAN, YOU SUPPOSE TO BE THE GOOD ONE WHAT YOU DO?"

"IT'S NOT HIM," I DECLARE. "KUE'S DEAD."

TAKING A STEP BACK AFTER LETTING ME GO, SALEEM STARES AT ME IN DISBELIEF. WE GRAB A BOOTH WITH A VIEW OF THE PARKING LOT, PREFERRED BY CHRIS, AND ORDER A ROUND OF COFFEE. OVER OUR SIMPLE BREAKFAST, I DETAIL THE EVENTS THAT OCCURRED FROM BEGINNING TO END. ONCE I FINISHED, CHRIS BEGAN.

"EVER SINCE I CAN REMEMBER, C-NOTE HAS BEEN A SNEAKY, SELFISH DELUSIONIST."

THAT'S A SUBTLE WAY OF PUTTING IT, I THINK TO MYSELF.

"WHICH IS WHY I CHOSE TO SIT BY THIS WINDOW, TO SEE IF EITHER ONE OF US WERE BEING FOLLOWED," HE CONTINUES. "I CHOSE THIS PLACE BECAUSE HE DOESN'T

TYPICALLY VENTURE INTO THE NORTHEAST, AND IF HE DOES SO, WE'LL KNOW WHY."

"WHY?" ASKS SALEEM.

"FOR HER, OF COURSE," CHRIS DIRECTS HIS ATTENTION TO ME, "OR IN THE LEAST, TRYING TO GET TO HER THROUGH ONE OF US. WHICH IS WHY I SUGGEST YOU GO SOMEWHERE WHERE YOU CAN LIE LOW FOR A WHILE"

"A SAFE HOUSE," I MUMBLE.

"EXACTLY."

BUT SALEEM WAS QUICK TO BE ON THE DEFENSIVE. "NAW, FUCK THAT I MESSED UP ENOUGH AS IT IS. YOU COMING WITH ME. THAT WAY I'LL KNOW YOU'LL BE SAFE."

"A SAFE HOUSE IS THE ONLY WAY, IF WE ARE TO COME UP WITH A PLAN THAT WILL SET C-NOTE STRAIGHT," CHRIS COUNTERED.

MORE

SALEEM NODS HIS HEAD, TAKING HEED TO WHAT CHRIS SAID AS I ASK HIM, "HOW DID YOU MESS UP?

"I KNEW SOMETHING WASN'T RIGHT WITH HOMEBOY, I JUST COULDN'T PUT MY FINGER ON IT. AND, IN YOUR OWN WAY, YOU TOLD ME THAT SOMETHING WAS UP, BUT I COULDN'T DO ANYTHING ABOUT IT WITHOUT KNOWING EXACTLY WHAT WAS GOING ON. I JUST WISH YOU TOLD ME WHAT WAS UP FROM JUMP STREET."

"WELL, NOWS YOUR CHANCE," CHRIS SUGGESTS.

SALEEM ASKS US TO ORDER SOMETHING WITH HIM CLAIMING THAT HE DOES HIS BEST THINKING WHILE EATING. I ORDER A FRENCH ONION SOUP WITH EXTRA GARLIC BREAD AND A RASPBERRY ICED TEA. WHAT CHRIS DIDN'T ORDER, IT SEEMED LIKE SALEEM DID.

THEY CAME UP WITH COUNTLESS POSSIBLITIES OF THEIR RETRIBUTION, THE MORE SINISTER AND GRUESOME, SURPRISINGLY COMING FROM CHRIS. AS I

PICKED FROM OUR BUFFET, SINCE NONE OF US WAS SATISFIED WITH WHAT WE INDIVIDUALLY ORDERED, THE ONLY CONCLUSION I WAS AWARE THEY HAD MADE WAS OF NO COPS. WHEN IT CAME DOWN TO MY INPUT AS TO WHERE MY SAFE HOUSE WOULD BE, NO DEBATE WAS NECESSARY. MISS ZUICKS.

CHAPTER 16

I ENTER THE FIRST GLASS DOOR JUST AS SOMEONE WAS EXITING THE SECOND SECURE DOOR. THE ONE YOU WOULD NEED TO HAVE A KEY OR BE BUZZED THROUGH BY A RESIDENT TO ENTER. THANKFULLY, THE LADY RECOGNIZED ME AND HELD IT OPEN. LOOKING AT THE SCENARIO ON THE BRIGHT SIDE, I CAN'T WAIT TO SEE THE SURPRISE ON MISS ZUICK'S FACE AFTER MY ABRUPT DEPARTURE. THAT IS, OF COURSE, BEFORE SHE FINDS OUT WHY I LEFT, AND THE NEED FOR MY RETURN.

AS MY SECOND KNOCK GOES UNANSWERED, THE LAUNDRY DOOR, AT THE END OPENS, OUT WALKS, NEARLY HOBBLING, AN ELDERLY WOMAN WITH A SHOPPING CART FULL OF NEATLY FOLDED LAUNDRY. SHE SAYS, "YOU'RE NOT GOING TO GET AN ANSWER FROM THAT DOOR."

TURNING TO HER, I ASK, "WHY, DID SHE MOVE?"

"MOVED ON IS MORE LIKE IT."

AT CLOSER INSPECTION, AS THE WOMAN COMES CLOSER, I INQUIRE, "I SEE YOU HAVEN'T. STILL KNOWING EVERYTHING THAT GOES ON IN THESE PARTS, HUNH?"

"HUMPH, I AIN'T GOING *ANY* WHERE UNLESS I WANNA GO. AND IT'S MY *JOB* TO KNOW WHAT BE GOING ONS. WHAT'S IT TO YOU ANYWAYS, WHAT ARE YOU, THE NEIGHBORHOOD WATCH?"

I BLOCK HER PATH AND SHE STOPS, MUMBLINHG UNDER HER BREATH. WHEN SHE LIFTS HER HEAD AND PUTS HER GLASSES ON, SHE SAYS, "WELL, AIN'T THAT

MORE

SOMETHING? I SHOULD OF KNOWN, WITH YOUR SMART MOUTH. GO ON AND OPEN THE DOOR FOR ME NOW, CHILD, I'M TIRED. PLAYING ALL THE TIME. I GOT SOMETHING FOR YOU."

NOT KNOWING WHETHER TO TAKE HER SERIOUSLY OR NOT, I DO AS SHE REQUESTS. MS JONES HAS NEVER GOTTEN ANYTHING FOR ANYONE, FROM WHAT I REMEMBER. ADDING TO MY ASTONISHMENT, HER APARTMENT WAS SOMEWHAT TIDY. WITH ONLY TWO PILES OF NEWSPAPERS, MAGAZINES AND JUNK MAIL SHE FEELS MIGHT COME IN HANDY ONE DAY, I AM PLEASANTLY SURPRISED.

BUT STILL, OLD HABITS DIE HARD, I GUESS. I TAKE THE CART FROM HER AND BEGIN TO PUT THEM AWAY, SHE INSTRUCTS, "DON'T PUT MY NIGHTIES UP TOO HIGH EITHER."

TAKING A SEAT WITH HER ON THE COUCH, SHE ASKS, "SO WHAT BRINGS YOU BACK AROUND THESE

PARTS? IT CERTAINLY AIN'T NO COINCIDENCE I RAN INTO YOU?"

HAVING A POINT, I TRY TO GIVE HER JUST A GIST OF THE SITUATION. ME NEEDING A PLACE TO STAY FOR A WHILE, BUT HER INCREDULOUS LOOK LETS ME KNOW IT ISN'T GOING TO BE THAT EASY.

"GOT YOURSELF IN SOME TROUBLE? YOU AIN'T ONE TO BE DABBLING IN NOTHING ILLEGAL SO IT MUST BE A BOY."

"PRETTY MUCH."

"SAME ONE THAT TOOK MY AID?"

AT THE RECOGNITION OF HER CLAIM TO ME, THE ONLY BIT OF CARE OR AFFECTION SOMEONE WOULD GET OUT OF HER, I INWARDLY SMILE, "YEAH."

"I'M HUNGRY," SHE STATES AND PICKS UP THE REMOTE, CHANGING THE CHANNEL.

IF I DIDN'T KNOW HER, I WOULDN'T HAVE KNOWN HOW TO TAKE HER RESPONSE. YET, FEEL COMFORTED IN HER SUBTLE WAY OF LETTING ME KNOW THAT EVERYTHINGS GOING TO BE ALL RIGHT. DURING OUR SIMPLE LUNCH OF TURKEY AND CHEESE SANDWICHES, SHE EXPLAINS HOW SHE REFUSED TO HAVE ANY FURTHER AIDES AFTER I LEFT, OPTING TO DO IT ALL HERSELF. WELL, TRY TO ANYWAY. SHE GOES ON TO EXPLAIN OF HOW AFTER I LEFT, MIZZ ZUICK COULDN'T STOP BLABBERING OF HER WORRYING OF MY WELL BEING JUST BEFORE SHE PASSED.

"THERE WASN'T A MINUTE I COULD GET ALONE FROM HER CONSTANTLY BEING AT MY DOOR ASKING IF I HAD HEARD ANYTHING. AND GOD FORBID, I STEP FOOT OUT OF MY DOOR. I COULD NEVER GET A WORD IN, SO I JUST KEPT IT MOVING."

YEAH, YOU NEVER LIKED A PERSON WHO COULD TALK MORE THAN YOU, I CONTEMPLATED SAYING BUT HELD MY TONGUE. I CAN'T START GOING IN ON HER LIKE I

MORE

USED TO, ESPECIALLY NOW, SINCE I NEED A PLACE TO STAY.

"I GIVE HER CREDIT, SHE WAS ONE SMART COOKIE. ONE DAY, I WAS IN HERE WATCHING MY STORIES AND A KNOCK CAME AT MY DOOR. I TRIED TO IGNORE IT, BUT IT WAS SO DISTRACTING THAT I GOT SO FRUSTRATED AND ANSWERED, NEARLY TAKING THE DOOR OFF ITS HINGES. YOU KNOW HOW I DON'T LIKE ANYONE INTERRUPTING MY STORIES. LILY STOOD AT MY OPEN DOOR WITH SUCH A SAD LOOK THAT THERE WASN'T AN ONUCE OF ME THAT COULD LET HER FEEL THE WRATH OF MY FURY. BARGING RIGHT PAST ME, SHE PLACES A BOX ON THE FLOOR," MS JONES POINTS TO IT IN THE CORNER. "SHE TOLD ME I WAS TO GIVE IT TO YOU, IF SOMETHING WAS TO EVER HAPPEN TO HER. DON'T YOU KNOW, THAT VERY NEXT DAY, SHE WAS FOUND DEAD IN HER APARTMENT, WENT IN HER SLEEP TOO. NOBODY WOULD HAVE EVER KNOWN EITHER IF IT WEREN'T FOR HER GROCERIES BEING DELIVERED. THE BOY DIDN'T GET AN ANSWER, SO HE CALLED THE

MORE

SUPER. THAT WAS THE 4TH OF JULY. GUESS SHE WENT OUT WITH A BANG."

I GO OVER TO THE LARGE SHIPPING BOX THAT'S USUALLY USED FOR WHEN PEOPLE MOVED. MY NAME INTRICATELY PRINTED ON THE TOP. "HAVEN'T TOUCHED IT EITHER, DIDN'T HAVE A REASON TO. DEFINITELY DIDN'T KNOW HOW TO CONTACT YOU. LILY SAID SHE HAD ALREADY TRIED WITH THE COMPANY, BUT THEY SAID THEY COULDN'T GIVE ANY PERSONAL INFORMATION."

I LOOK AROUND FOR A PLACE TO SIT WITH THE BOX AND MS JONES TO TAKE IT IN HER ROOM. ONCE THERE, I SET THE HEAVY BOX DOWN WONDERING HOW MISS ZUICK COULD HAVE CARRIED IT. WITH MY NAIL, I SPLIT THE MASKING TAPE AT THE SEAM OF THE FLAPS ON THE BOX. A LETTER WAS PROMINENTLY LAID ATOP THE BOXES CONTENTS.

MY DEAREST YANI,

THE REASONS WHY YOU HLS LEFT, LEFT ME PERTURBED, BUT UNDOUBTEDLY, THEY MUST URGENTLY REALISTIC. I AM INDEED APOLOGETIC IN THE SENSE YOU DID NOT FEEL THE NEED FOR ME TO ASSIST YOU IN YOUR WOES. ALSO IN THE FACT THAT I WAS NOT ABLE TO PRESENT THESE ITEMS TO YOU ME. I FELT MY TIME COMING AND HONESTLY, MORE WORRIED FOR YOU SAKE, THEN MY OWN.

I WANT YOU TO KNOW THAT YOU ARE VERY SPECIAL TO ME AND BROUGHT MUCH JOY TO MY HEART. FROM OUR INITIAL HELLO, MY HEART WARMED AND OPENED TO YOU. YOU COULD HAVE NEVER BEEN JUST MY AIDE, BUT IN MY VIEW, A DAUGHTER. I PRAYED PERSISTENTLY THAT THE LORD WOULD GRACE YOU WITH HIS PRESENCE AND PROVE TO YOU THAT WITH HIS ASSISTANCE; YOU HAVE THE STRENGHT AND COURAGE TO OVERCOME ANY OBSTACLE THAT MAY STAND IN YOUR WAY.

MORE

THE THINGS IN THIS BOX IS SOME OF MY MOST PRIZED POSSESSIONS AND WHAT I FELT WOULD BE MOST BENEFICIAL TO YOU. I HOPE, THEY WILL COME IN HANDY.

--REMEMBER, WHOSE LIFE YOU ARE LIVING? WHAT PURPOSES ARE YOU LIVING IT FOR? AND, ARE YOU GETTING ALL YOU ARE SUPPOSING TO, OUT OF IT?"

-WITH DEEP AFFECTION,

LILY ZUICK

LOOKING BACK AT THE BOX, I WONDER WHAT SHE COULD HAVE POSSIBLY LEFT ME. I WASN'T EXPECTING ANYTHING, AND CERTAINLY DON'T REMEMBER HER MENTIONING INCLUDING ME IN HER WILL. BUT, THEN AGAIN, THE LITTLE SHE DID HAVE, SHE DIDN'T HAVE ANY FAMILY TO LEAVE IT TO IN THE FIRST PLACE. PICKING UP THE KING JANES VERSION OF THE BIBLE, I NOTICE AN ENVELOPE MARKING "PSALMS 23." COMFORTING, I THINK AS I OPEN THE ENVELOPE EXPECTING ANOTHER LETTER, SOMETHING SHE MIGHT HAVE FORGOTTEN TO WRITE IN

MORE

THE FIRST. MY SUSPICIONS WERE WRONG AS I PULL OUR

A CHECK FOR $250,000. ASIDE FROM THE ANTIQUE WATCH, A

GOLD CRUCIFIX AND CHAIN, EARRINGS, PEARLS, AND

RING. HER VERY OWN COOKBOOK, I AM AT A LOST OF

WHAT TO DO WITH IT ALL, ESPECIALLY, THE MONEY.

"MISS ZUICK," I SAY SOFTLY, LOOKING UP TO

HEAVEN. "YOU ARE QUITE A WOMAN."

CHAPTER 17

FOR THE NEXT FEW DAYS, MY THOUGHTS SHIFT

BETWEEN THE MONEY MISS ZUICK LEFT, AND NOT

HEARING FROM CHRIS NOR SALEEM. ON THE FOURTH

DAY, I GET TIRED OF WASHING OUT THE SAME CLOTHES

EVERY MORNING AND CALL SALEEM. AFTER THREE

RINGS, HIS PHONE IS ANSWERED. NO ONE SAYS

ANYTHING, SO NEITHER DO I. A MINUTE WENT BY BEFORE

HE ASKED WHO IT WAS.

MORE

"SCREENING YOUR CALLS AGAIN?"

"OH, WHAT'S UP, HOW YOU HOLDING UP?" HE ASKS.

"I'M ALRIGHT, BUT I NEED SOME CLOTHES."

TALKING TO SOMEONE IN THE BACKGROUND, WHEN HE COMES BACK, "TOYA GONNA GET YOU SOME STUFF WHEN SHE GOES OUT, AFTER I GET SOME SLEEP, WHEN ME AND CHRIS SWITCH OUR TWELVE HOUR SHIFTS AT 6, WE'LL BRING 'EM THROUGH AND HOLLA AT YOU THEN, AIGHT?"

TWELVE HOUR SHIFTS, I THINK. "OKAY." I HANG UP. WOE, THEY REALLY LOOKING FOR THIS DUDE AND IT'S ALL BECAUSE OF ME. KUE'S DEATH, BECAUSE OF ME. I WAS READY TO CALL SALEEM BACK AND TELL HIM NOT TO EVEN BOTHER. I DIDN'T WANT ANYONE ONE ELSE GETTING HURT BECAUSE OF ME.

COMING OUT OF THE BATHROOM, MS. JONES ASKS, "YOU NEVER SAID WHAT LILY LEFT."

MY MIND RACES TO THE LAST LINE OF HER LETTER, "WHOSE LIFE ARE YOU LIVING; AND FOR WHAT PURPOSE?" IT WAS THAT WHICH MADE ME SEE THAT I CAN'T GO ON LIVING MY LIFE IN HIDING, IN FEAR.

I PICK UP MISS ZUICK'S BIBLE AND IT OPENS TO ONE OF ITS TAGGED PAGES. THE HIGHLIGHTED PORTION READS AS FOLLOWS: "AN EYE FOR AN EYE, TOOTH FOR TOOTH." I SHARE THIS WITH MS. JONES WHO COULDN'T THINK OF A BETTER PASSAGE. SHE THEN ASKS ME DO I TALK TO MYSELF A LOT. WHEN I ASKED HER WHAT WOULD MAKE HER SAY SOMETHING LIKE THAT, SHE REPLIES THAT SHE OVERHEARD ME IN THE BATHROOM DOING HER MORNING REGIME. I EXPLAINED THAT I WAS SPEAKING TO MY BROTHER AND HOW HE WAS GOING TO DROP ME OFF SOME CLOTHES LATER ON.

IF I KNEW SHE WAS GOING TO SNAP OUT ABOUT IT, I WOULD HAVE MADE OTHER PLANS. WHEN I TRIED TO EXPLAIN THAT I WOULD, "OH NO, THAT'S FINE. I JUST THOUGHT A LITTLE CONSIDERATION WOULD HAVE BEEN

MORE

NICE. YOU KNOW, ASKED ME FIRST. THAT'S ALL. I DON'T GET VISITORS TO OFTEN. WHAT AM I GOING TO WEAR?"

WE END UP SKIPPING BREAKFAST AND AFTER THREE HOURS OF MATCHING, MIXING AND MISMATCHING EVERY SINGLE ITEM OF CLOTHING SHE OWNED, NOTHING SEEMED TO BE GOOD ENOUGH. AT ELEVEN A.M. I TRY TO CONVINCE HER THAT IT'LL ONLY BE MY BROTHER AND A GOOD FRIEND, NOBODY IMPORTANT, SHE JUST WOULD NOT LET IT GO.

SETTLING ON A WHITE BLOUSE AND FLORAL ANKLE LENGTH SKIRT, THAT SHE PULLED TO BELOW HER BOSOM, STILL REACHES HER ANKLES SHE ANXIOUSLY AWAITS THE VISITORS AS IF THEY WERE THE DUKE AND DUTCHESS OF CAMBRIDGE COMING TO PERSONALLY VISIT HER. WE COULD NOT GET THROUGH A FULL HOUR OF A MEDEA MOVIE, HER FAVORITES WITHOUT HER ASKING, "WHAT ARE THEY LIKE? WHEN ARE THEY GETTING HERE? DO YOU THINK THEY'LL STAY FOR DINNER?"

MORE

AS THE AFTERNOON BEGAN TO PROGRESS INTO EARLY EVENING, I GUESS HER PATIENCE RAN OUT FROM WAITING AND SHE CHANGED BACK INTO HER MUMU. MS. JONES ASKES WHAT WERE WE GOING TO HAVE FOR DINNER AND I SO WASN'T IN THE MOOD TO COOK, I ORDER FROM ONE OF THE LOCAL PIZZIARIAS. NIPPING HER OBJECTIONS OF CHEESESTEAKS AND CHEESE FRIES BEING TOO GREASEY, IN THE BUD, I TELL HER THAT SHE CAN AFFORD THE SPLURGE. THANKFULLY I KNEW THE NUMBER ON MY BANK CARD BY HEART, WHICH I ONLY USE IN EMERGENCIES OR CASES SUCH AS THIS WHEN I DON'T HAVE MONEY ON HAND.

BUT I SOON LEARN, SOME EMERGENCIES, MONEY JUST CAN'T BUY YOUR WAY OUT OF.

CHAPTER 18

STRUGGLING TO BREATHE AS MY THROAT GETS CONSTRICTED, TIGHTER AND TIGHTER, MY EYES PLEADS FCR RELIEF. FROZEN WITH SHOCK, I AM UNABLE TO DO ANYTHING TO SAVE MY OWN LIFE. FILLED WITH RAGE, THE LOOK OF PURE HATRED AND DISGUST, MY ASSAILANT SPITS, "YOU JUST GONNA RUN AWAY FROM ME LIKE THAT? AFTER I POURED OUT MY HEART TO YOU? YOU THINK THAT THIS SHIT IS A GAME? HUNH? DO YOU?" HE SCREAMS AS HIS GRIP TIGHTENS EVEN FURTHER AROUND MY NECK, MY LIFE NEARING ITS END, THE HAPPIEST TIMES FILL MY VISION.

WHEN I FIRST LEARNED HOW TO RIDE MY BIKE; MY ACCEPTANCE TO MY CREATIVE ARTS CHARTER SCHOOL; RECEIVING MY AWARD FOR THE MOST MEMORABLE PERFORMANCE, AS WELL AS MY DIPLOMA AT GRADUATION. SUDDENLY, AIR FILLS MY PASSAGE WAYS AT THE SOUND OF A MUFFELED THUMP. C-NOTE SWEARS PS HE LETS GO OF MY THROAT TO RUB THE BACK OF HIS HEAD.

MORE

QUICKLY MOVING AWAY FROM HIM, MY HAND REPLACES HIS AS I MASSAGE MY SORE THROAT, TAKING IN VAST, BUT SHALLOW BREATHS. AS I DID SO, I NOTICE MS. JONES STANDING BEHIND C-NOTE, RAISING THE 10 INCH CAST IRON SKILLET AGAIN. IT COMES DOWN ON HIS LEFT SHOULDER AND HE CRIES OUT IN AGONY.

"NOT IN MY HOUSE YOU LITTLE GOOD FOR NOTHING PIP SQUEAK. ONLY ONE DOSING OUT DAMAGE IN *THIS* HOUSE IS ME!" MS. JONES DECLARES AS SHE RAISES HER ARMS AGAIN.

AT THE ALL TOO FAMILIAR GESTURE, DO I DIVE IN BETWEEN THE TWO OF THEM JUST AS A LOUD POP SOUNDS. LYING IN SEARING PAIN, A POOL OF BLOOD BEGINS TO FORM AROUND ME ON THE FLOOR JUST AS THE FRONT DOOR OF THE APARTMENT GETS KICKED IN. RAPID GUNFIRE SOUNDS UNTIL IT IS REPLACED BY A CLICKING SIGNIFYING THAT THE CHAMBERS ARE EMPTY.

MORE

A BODY SLUMPS BEHIND ME, GURGLING AS I HEAR TWO FAMILIAR VOICES AS I BEGAN BLACKENING OUT, BUT MY ONLY CONCERN WAS IF MS. JONES WAS OKAY.

CHAPTER 19

WAKING FROM A RESTFUL SLEEP, THE FIRST THING THAT GRABS MY ATTENTION IS AN UNFAMILIAR WEIGHT ON MY HAND. AS I GAZE AT THE SHINY YELLOW OBJECT, I REALIZE THAT FIRST, I DIDN'T GO TO SLEEP WITH IT ON. SECONDLY, IT WASN'T THE RING MISS ZUICK HAD LEFT ME. MY GAZE TRAVELS UP MY LEFT ARM TO THE TUBES PLACED IN THEM, CONNECTING ME TO A MACHINE. AUTOMATICALLY, I SIT UP. THE HEART MONITOR BEEPS A BIT QUICKER.

"EASY THERE, SUPERWOMAN."

I LOOK TO MY RIGHT AND CHRIS IS SITTING IN AN ARMCHAIR WITH A HALF-HEARTED SMILE.

"HOW ARE YOU FEELING?" HE ASKS.

"I'M FINE. WHY?"

"A LOT HAS HAPPENED IN THE PAST TWO WEEKS YOU WERE IN A COMA NOT TO MENTION, THE FEW SCARES YOU GAVE US."

"COMA?" REMEMBERING EVERYTHING UP UNTIL I BLACKED OUT, CHRIS FILLS ME IN ON WHAT I MISSED. APPARENTLY, HE AND SALEEM HAD KILLED C-NOTE THAT NIGHT AND IF IT HADN'T BEED FOR ME, TAKING THAT BULLET FOR MS. JONES, SHE MIGHT HAVE PERISHED AS WELL.

UNFORTUNATELY, THE BULLET ENTERED MY ABDOMEN INSTANTLY KILLING THE EIGHT-WEEK-OLD FETUS I DIDN'T KNOW I WAS CARRYING. TAKING HIS BABY WITH HIM, EVEN THOUGH I DON'T BELIEVE IN ABORTIONS, I'M RELIEVED TO KNOW I AM NO LONGER

CARRYING C-NOTE'S BABY. AFTER INVESTIGATING, THE POLICE SUSPECTED THAT THE REASON HE FOUND ME IS BECAUSE HE REPORTED MY BANK CARD STOLEN AND ONCE HE WAS NOTIFIED OF ITS LAST PURCHASE, HE GOT INTO CONTACT WITH THE PIZZA PLACE.

DUE TO THE AMOUNT OF BLOOD I LOSS, IS WHY I HAD SLIPPED INTO A COMA; MY BODY HAVING TO REVITALIZE AND STABILIZE ITSELF AND RECOVER FROM THE LOSS OF THE BABY, AND FOR MY WOMB TO HEAL. THE DOCTORS TOLD CHRIS AND SALEEM THAT AFTER MY EMERGENCY SURGERY, I MIGHT NOT BE ABLE TO HAVE CHILDREN AGAIN, YET CHRIS COMFORTS THAT ONLY TIME WILL TELL.

I ASK, "WHERE'S SALEEM? WHERE'S MS. JONES? HOW IS SHE?"

"MS JONES IS FINE. SHE WAS RELEASED AFTER HER OBSERVATION STAY, WHICH I HIGHLY DOUBT THE DOCTORS COULD KEEP HER ANY LONGER, EVEN IF THEY

MORE

WANTED TO. UNFORTUNATELY, HER APARTMENT IS NO LONGER AVAILABLE TO HER, SO SHE's AT MY HOUSE UNTIL WE FIND HER ANOTHER PLACE. HER LANDLORD EVICTED HER DUE TO HER CAUSING AN UNSAFE LIVING ENVIRONMENT FOR THE OTHER TENANTS. OR SO HE CLAIMS."

"SHE CAN STAY WITH ME," I REPLY WITHOUT A THOUGHT, BUT WITH CONVICTION. "SHE DESERVES IT. AT LEAST I OWE HER THAT MUCH."

"THAT'S FINE, SHE CAN STAY WITH US," CHRIS SAYS. "SALEEM IS RUNNING HIS THREE MILES. HE'S BEEN DOING THAT EVER SINCE YOU BEEN IN HERE." IN A SOMBER NOTE, HE SAYS "SALEEM STILL FEELS RESPONSIBLE, EVEN MORE SO, BEING AS THOUGH OUR ATTEMPTS AT THE SAFE HOUSE LANDED YOU IN HERE. ACTUALLY, HE SHOULD BE BACK IN A FEW MINUTES. HE USUALLY COMES JUST BEFORE THE DOCTOR MAKES HIS ROUNDS."

MORE

TAKING IN MY SURROUNDINGS ONCE AGAIN, WITH THE INFORMATION HE JUST GAVE ME, NEVER IMAGINED ME NEEDING TO BE IN A HOSPITAL. I NOTICE A PORTRAIT OF A COUPLE JUMPING THE BROOM ON A BEACH WITH THE BLUEST WATER I HAVE EVER SEEN. JUST BELOW, THE CAPTION READS: "THE DOOR TO POSSIBILITIES, IF ONLY YOU'LL OPEN IT BY SAYING 'YES'." THE UNDERTONE TUGS AT MY HEARTSTRINGS, BUT I CANNOT FIGURE OUT WHY.

"WHAT DO YOU THINK?"

"OF?" I ASK.

"YOUR RING," CHRIS CLEARIFUES.

THE WEIGHT GAINS A POUND; IT SEEMS LIKE, AS I LIFT MY HAND TO ADMIRE IT. "IT'S BEAUTIFUL."

"SO IS THE ONE WHO IS WEARING IT."

"MAN, I KNEW YOU COULDN'T WAIT," SALEEM SAYS ENTERING THE ROOM. "YOU WERE SUPPOSED TO WAIT TILL I GOT BACK TO PROPOSE."

"I DID WAIT. I DIDN'T ASK."

"OH, MY BAD." SALEEM KISSES ME ON MY FOREHEAD. "GLAD YOU'RE UP. YOU DON'T KNOW HOW BADLY I WANTED TO TALK TO YOU."

"YOU DID TALK TO HER. THE WHOLE TIME, I MIGHT ADD," CHRIS STATES. "WHAT'S THE USE OF YOU CALLING HER LIL G, IF YOU DON'T HAVE ANY FAITH IN HER TO BE, A LIL GANGSTER?"

"UH, HOLD UP GUYS. YOU TWO ARE MOVING JUST A LITTLE BIT TO FAST FOR ME RIGHT NOW. OBVIOUSLY, YOU TWO HAVE HAD YOUR LITTLE BUDDY-BUDDY TIME TO DISCUSS IT, BUT CAN I JOIN IN ON THIS CONVERSATION ABOUT A PROPOSAL?"

"WHAT'S THERE TO DISCUSS? YOU TWO ARE PERFECT FOR EACH OTHER EVEN I KNOW THAT." SALEEM SAYS.

"YEAH, BUT-"

"YOU HAVEN'T TAKEN THE RING OFF," CHRIS COMMENTS.

"OK, BUT THAT DOESN'T MEAN—"

SALEEM INTERJECTS, "YOU LOVE HIM, RIGHT?"

I LOOK FROM SALEEM, TO CHRIS, TO MY RING. "I DO, BUT IT JUST CAN'T BE THAT SIMPLE, CAN IT?"

"IT CAN BE AS SIMPLE AS YOU WANT IT TO BE," CHRIS COMFORTS

AS THE DOCTOR STEPS IN, SHE GREETS US WITH A PLEASANT VOICE, FACE PLASTERED IN MY FILE.

CLOSING IT, SHE STARES DIRECTLY AT ME. SHOCK, I RECOGNIZE, BUT AS TO WHY SHE SUDDENLY STORMED OUT, WAS A MYSTERY TO ME.

MORE

"WHAT'S WRONG WITH HER?" I ASK.

"DON'T KNOW, BUT THAT'S NOT YOUR NORMAL DOCTOR," CHRIS ADMITS.

SALEEM FOLLOWS WITH, "MAYBE SHE WAS SURPRISED THE LIL SOLDIER PULLED THROUGH."

A MOMENT PASSED BEFORE ANOTHER DOCTOR ENTERS; HAPPY I PULLED OUT OF MY COMA. HE ASKS ME A BUNCH OF QUESTIONS FOR HIS MENTAL EXAM, MY NAME, AGE, AND SO FORTH. AFTER PHYSICALLY EXAMING ME, POKING AND PRODING, HE EXPLAINS HE'S ORDERING SOME TEST TO SEE HOW I'M HEALING INTERNALLY; A SERIES OF STANDARD PROTOCOL.

WHEN HE ASKED IF WE HAD ANY QUESTIONS FOR HIM, THERE WAS ONLY ONE, YET WE ALL POUNCED ON HIM AS IF WE WERE HUNGRY ARCTIC WOLVES, IN THE DEAD OF WINTER, READILY BECOMING CANNABILIST IF HE HADN'T WANDERED BY.

TRYING TO LAUGH OFF THE ATTACK, I CUT HIM SHORT BY ASKING, "DID SHE LEAVE BECAUSE SHE RECOGNISES ME? BECAUSE I MOST CERTAINLY RECOGNIZE HER."

CHAPTER 20

SEEING AS THOUGH I WOULD NOT RELENT, REGARDLESS OF MY CONDITION, DUE TO THE PROBABILITY THE TRUTH WOULD BE BENEFICIAL TO MY HEALTH, THEY GET THE DISAPPEARING DOCTOR TO EXPLAIN HERSELF.

"MY NAME IS COPPERFIELD, NOW. DR. EVELYN COPPERFIELD." DEFEATEDLY, SHE SIGHS. "EVERYTHING WAS PERFECT. I DON'T KNOW WHERE TO LOOK FOR THE CAUSE OF THE PROBLEM, YET SUDDENLY, THERE IT WAS. I WAS A FAIRLY GOOD STUDENT. I WAS PART OF THE

ROBOTICS TEAM, STUDENT COUNCIL, AND SAFETY PATROL THROUGHOUT MIDDLE AND HIGH SCHOOL. I WOULDN'T HAVE CALLED MYSELF 'POPULAR' BACK IN THOSE DAYS, BUT I WOULD SAY THAT A LOT OF PEOPLE KNEW ME; I WAS WELL LIKED.

"ONE DAY AT LUNCH, A FEW GIRLS WERE TRYING TO FIGURE OUT IF MY HAIR WAS ACTUALLY MINES, OR AN EXTENTION, DARING THIS NEW KID TO TEST IT OUT. LONG STORY SHORT, IT WAS AN EXTENTION AND I RAN AWAY CRYING. WHAT, I DIDN'T KNOW, WAS THIS GUY PICKED UP MY PONYTAIL, AND WALKED AROUND ALL DAY, LOOKING FOR ME TO GIVE IT BACK.

SKIPPING SCHOOL FOR THE REST OF THE DAY, WHEN I HAD RETURNED TO SCHOOL THE NEXT DAY THAT GUY WAS WAITING FOR ME AT MY LOCKER, *WITH* MY HAIR EXTENSIONS IN HIS HANDS.

"YO, THIS YOURS AIN'T IT?" HE ASKED THRUSTING IT TOWARDS ME.

MORE

"WHY, WHAT'S IT TO YOU?"

"CUZ I'M GIVING IT BACK. WHAT IT LOOK LIKE? IT AIN'T MINE."

AT THE MOST OPPORTUNE TIME DID A GROUP OF GIRLS WALK BY AND GIGGLE. I KNEW YESTERDAYS FIASCO WOULD HAVE SPREAD LIKE A WILDFIRE, BUT I NEVER FELT SHAME AND EMBARASSMENT LIKE THAT BEFORE.

"YO, YA'LL GOT A PROBLEM WIT MY GIRL?" HE ASKS THEM AS HE PUTS HIS ARM AROUND MY SHOULDER.

"I WAS FLABBERGASTED. FIRST, FOR THIS GUY I'VE NEVER MET, STANDING UP FOR ME, CLAIMING ME AND THEN, ALL THE GIRLS APOLOGIZED AND WENT ON THEIR WAY. SOON THEREAFTER, I WAS PRIVILEGED TO FIND OUT WHY. YOU SEE, IN MY LIFE, I NEVER HUNG OUT WITH THE BAD CRCWD AND QUITE HONESTLY, I WAS THE EPITOME OF ANYTHING BAD. HOWEVER, HE WAS A TOTALLY DIFFERENT STORY, DOING A SHORT STINT AT

Juvie over the summer. The only reason he had gotten into such a prestigious chartered school was because His father was the mayor who contributed a sizeable donation for his son to get a good education.

"From the moment my parents met him, just before we went to prom, they disapproved of him. They knew who he was by his reputation, and his family, and needless to say, they wanted better for me. What they didn't know was he and I was already an established couple, that night being when I gave him, myself completely.

"I tried to conceal my pregnancy from my parents for as long as I could, yet they found out and tried to force me to have an abortion. After the continuous reminders, of how my actions were of such a disappointment, of how they knew he was no good for me and of how my fathers reputation as the then, Philadelphia's

More

SCHOOL DISTRICT'S SUPERINTENDENT WAS PUT INTO

JEOPARDY BY MY ACTIONS; NO LONGER ABLE TO DEAL

WITH MY PARENTS I LEFT HOME.

"THE MAYOR TRIED T0 EASE THE ILL WILL WITH

FATHER AND TRIED TO GET HIM TO SEE THAT MY

PREGNANCY SHOULD BRIDGE THE GAP OF THEIR LIFE

LONG FUED. MY FATHER WAS A STUBBORN MAN AND THE

APPEAL TO CITY HALL, THE MONTH PRIOR, FOR MORE

SCHOOL FUNDING MUST HAVE INSULTED HIM BITTERLY

GETTING DENIED SINCE NONE OF US HAVE SPOKEN TO

HIM SINCE THAT DAY.

CHAPTER 21

"WE LIVED COMFORTABLY FOR A WHILE AFTER

THAT. ME, MY NEWLYWED HUSBAND AND OUR

BUSTLING BABY BOY. THE MAYOR HAD GIVEN US A

TOWNHOUSE ADJACENT TO THE RECENTLY FINISHED

HOUSING PROJECT AND HIS SON, WHO WAS ADAMANT ABOUT *NOT* ATTENDING COLLEGE, A JOB IN WASTE MANAGEMENT. I ALWAYS DREAMED OF HAVING A CAREER, BUT THAT WAS BEFORE THESE EVENTS UNFOLDED. AT MY HUSBAND'S REQUEST, I BECAME A HOUSEWIFE AND STAY AT HOME MOTHER. BOY, DID I NEED THE TIME.

"WITH NO HELP, NOR KNOWLEDGE OF THE TWO, I HAD MY WORK CUT OUT FOR ME IN FIGURING OUT WHAT WAS WHAT. AS TIME WENT ON, THINGS BEGAN FALLING IN PLACE AND UNLIKE OUR FIRST CHILD, WE PLANNED ON HAVING ANOTHER. PLANNING WAS ALL THAT WAS NECESSARY AS THE FIRST ACTUAL PRACTICE OF INTERCOURSE PRODUCED ANOTHER SON. AS IF IT WERE YESTERDAY, I CAN STILL REMEMBER THEIR FACES. MY CHILD LIGHTING UP TO EXPLORE THE NEW WORLD WITH A VOICE THAT DEMANDED TO BE HEARD AND HIS FATHER, PROUD TO HAVE FATHERED ANOTHER SON.

MORE

"I WAS HAPPY, FOR THE MOST PART. OH, DO NOT MISTAKE ME, THE ABILITY GIVE AND BRING LIFE INTO THIS WORLD IS ASTONISHING, YET IN SECRET, I DESPERATELY WANTED A GIRL. IT'S JUST HOW I PICTURED LIFE: THE MARRIED LIFE. A BOY AND A GIRL, WITH LOVING CAREER DRIVEN PARENTS, BUT UNFORTUNATELY, NONE OF WHAT I INITIALLY DREAMED ABOUT, AS A YOUNG GIRL, CAME TO FRUITION.

"WITH A NEWBORN AND A FIVE-YEAR-OLD, NOT TO MENTION, A HUSBAND AND HOUSEHOLD TO CARE FOR, I PUT MY SELFISH DELUDE TO THE SIDE AND CARRIED ON WITH MY WOMANLY DUTIES. AS IF TO ADD INSULT TO INJURY, THE INFLATION IN THE COST OF LIVING, MY HUSBAND FACING LAY-OFFS, DUE TO AN EMINENT RECESSION, WHICH EXCITES ISSUES BETWEEN HIM AND I, I TAKE MY ELEVEN-MONTH-OLD TO THE HOSPITAL IN THE DEAD OF WINTER.

"FINALLY SEEN BY AN EMERGENCY ROOM PHYSICIAN, I EXPLAIN HIS FEVER, DIARRHEA, AND BOUT

MORE

OF CRYING SPELLS WHICH IS UNUSUAL FOR HIM. DURING THE DOCTORS EXAM, SYMPTOMS SEEM TO TAKE OVER ME AS I BEGAN VOMITING. FOR CAUTIONARY REASONS, THE DOCTOR TAKES BLOOD AND URINE SAMPLES FROM ME, AS WELL, TO SEE IF I HAD CONTRACTED MY SON'S ILLNESS, OR VICE VERSA.

"I DREADED THE TWO WEEKS AFTER THAT VISIT TO RECEIVE THE RESULTS OF OUR TESTS. THE THOUGHT OF ME GETTING MY OWN CHILD SICK IS WHAT SICKENED ME THE MOST. BEYOND MY OCCASIONAL VOMITING, PHYSICALLY, I FELT FINE. IT WAS MY PRIDE WHICH WAS WOUNDED. WHAT MOTHER WOULD PUT HER OWN CHILD'S HEALTH AT RISK? WHEN THE DAY WE WERE TO EXPECT THE RESULTS CAME, I WAS BESIDE MYSELF WITH LOATHING AND PITY. NONE THAT REFLECTED I SHOULD HAVE BEEN.

"THE RESULTS HAD COME TO PROVE THAT I WAS NOT TO BE BLAMED, DIRECTLY AT LEAST, FOR MY YOUNGEST SON TO CONTRACT PNEUMONIA, SINCE THAT

MORE

WASN'T THE CAUSE FOR MY UPSET STOMACH. WITH

HEARING THE NEWS OF BRINGING, YET ANOTHER CHILD

INTO THIS WORLD, EVERYTHING BEGAN TO SLOWLY SLIP

AWAY FROM US AS MY HUSBAND BEGAN CONFIDING

LESS AND LESS IN ME, AND MORE INTO HIS BOOZE.

"FARTHER ALONG THAN I HAD ANTICIPATED, A

FEW MONTHS LATER I GAVE BIRTH TO A LITTLE GIRL IN

APRIL WHO SUFFERED FROM JAUNDICE NOT KNOWING

HOW BAD THINGS COULD HAVE BEEN, I QUICKLY FIND

OUT THAT RAISING THREE CHILDREN ON MY OWN, WITH

HALF A PAYCHECK, WAS NOT THE LUXURY LIFE I ONCE

ENVISIONED.

"SOMEHOW, I MAINTAINED, MOVING ON AND

PUSHING THROUGH, BEING 'THEN, A MODERN-DAY

SINGLE MOTHER. RARELY, DID I RECEIVE ANY SORT OF

HELP FROM MY LIVE IN, DETACHED HUSBAND. USUALLY

ONLY COMING ON SUNDAYS DURING FOOTBALL SEASON

AS HE WOULD GIVE THE INS AND OUTS OF THE SPORT TO

OUR OLDEST SON. ONCE, WHEN I SUGGESTED THAT WE

MORE

ALL SIT DOWN AND ENJOY THE GAME AS A FAMILY, IT LED TO AN EXPLOSIVE OUTBURST, ON HIS BEHALF, MAKING IT KNOWN THAT HE DID WANT HIS FOOTBALL EXPERIENCES TO BE RUINED BY INTERRUPTIONS FROM TWO WHINY-NEEDY BRATS. HOW IT WOULD INTERFERE WITH MY *DUTIES* OF TAKING CARE OF THE KIDS, HIM, THE HOUSE, AND DINNER.

"ALTHOUGH HE DIDN'T PUT HIS HANDS ON ME, THAT NIGHT BEGAN TO FEAR, THAT THAT DAY WOULD BE COMING. THE SEED OF MY MARRIAGE BEGINNING TO FAIL HAD BEEN IMPLANTED AND THE THOUGHT OF MY FATHER BEING RIGHT, ALL THOSE YEARS AGO, BEGAN TO GNAW AT ME. THE CYCLE CONTINUED, UNFORTUNATELY, MY HUSBAND'S DRINKING, MY ATTEMPTING TO FIX, WHAT I WAS IN DENIAL OF BEING IRREPARABLE AND TRYING MY HARDEST TO ENSURE MY KIDS WEREN'T BEING AFFECTED BY BEING IN AN ALL TO STIGMATIZED URBAN AFRICAN AMERICAN BROKEN HOME. VERY LITTLE INCOME, A SHELL OF A FATHER, AND MY

MORE

HUSBAND WHO I HAD LONG LOST, YET STILL HELD OUT HOPE THAT HE WOULD ONE DAY RETURN.

CHAPTER 22

"A FEW YEARS HAD PASSED WITH NO LIGHTING TO SHOW ME A WAY. BUT, A DOOR EVENTUALLY OPENING AND I TOOK IT. AS WAS THE NORM, PAYDAY CAME AROUND AND HE WAS LATE COMING HOME. BY THE FOLLOWING MORNING WHEN I AWOKE ALONE IN BED, I CHECKED THE HOUSE, NOT FINDING HIM. I WAS WORRIED, YES, BUT NOT ALARMED. I FIGURED HE GOT WASTED AS USUAL AT HIS FAVORITE BAR AND PASSED OUT; WHEN HE SOBBERED UP, HE ALWAYS CAME HOME.

"IT DID STRIKE ME AS ODD THAT THIS TIME, HE DIDN'T. I BEGAN MAKING CALLS IN SEARCH OF HIM. WITH THE REFRIGERATOR BARE AND NO CLUE WHERE HE COULD POSSIBLY BE, MY CHILDRENS CRY OF HUNGER

MORE

DROVE ME TO A POINT, I NEVER DREAMED OF CONSIDERING. I SOLD MY BODY FOR A HUNDRED DOLLARS TO A GUY IN THE NEIGHBORHOOD KNOWN FOR HIS DEALINGS IN THE SEX TRADE.

"ASHAMED, DISGUSTED AND DISGRACED BY THE ACT I WAS FORCED TO COMMIT, I THOROUGHLY SCRUBBED MY BODY AFTERWARDS WITH NEARLY EVERY CLEANING AGENT WE HAD BEFORE I COULD EVEN ATTEMPT TO FIX A MEAL FOR MY CHILDREN. SENDING THEM TO BED FULL, I SET MYSELF UP IN THE LIVING ROOM WAITING FOR MY HUSBAND TO WALK THROUGH THE DOOR. ANGER AND SADNESS FILLING ME, MOMENT BY MOMENT AND I BURST INTO TEARS, NOT KNOWING HOW MY LIFE ENDED UP LIKE THIS.

"RAW AND NUMB FROM EMOTION, I JUMP AWAKE AS I FEEL I AM RELIVING THE HORRIBLE NIGHTMARE OF DAYS PAST. YET, TO ASTONISHMENT, IT WAS MY DISAPPEARING HUSBAND FORCING HIMSELF ON ME. WHEN I TRIED TO GET HIM TO STOP, HE PERSISTED

MORE

FURTHER. HE CLAIMED THAT HE WAS IN SUCH A GOOD MOOD; HE WANTED TO SHARE THE EXPERIENCE WITH ME. HITTING MY SPOT, I THOUGHT HE LONG SINCE FORGOTTEN, I GIVE IN. THANKING GOD THAT HE FINALLY CAME TO HIS SENSES. FINALLY GETTING BACK THE MAN I FELL IN LOVE WITH.

"THE RECONCILIATION WAS ALL TO SWEET, AS WE MADE LOVE AS NEVER BEFORE. THE SUN ROSE AND I WAS THE LAST TO FOLLOW. MY OLDEST, NOW TWELVE, TELLS ME THAT I HAD FORGOTTEN TO GET MILK YESTERDAY, AND DAD DIDN'T GET ANY AFTER GOING OUT THIS MORNING. I REACHED INTO MY POCKET TO SEND HIM TO THE STORE, YET IT WAS EMPTY. I SEARCHED AND SEARCHED. MY POCKETS, THE COUCH CUSHIONS, UNDERNEATH THE COUCH. NOTHING. I ASKED HIM IF HE SAW ANY MONEY LYING AROUND, I MAYBE MISPLACED.

"NO" WAS HIS RESPONSE BUT REFERENCING THAT I SHOULD ASK HIS FATHER, WHO WENT OUT AND BROUGHT SOMETHING.

MORE

I FIND MY HUSBAND IN OUR ROOM AND IS I OPENED THE DOOR FURTHER, IT CREAKED, STARTLING HIM UP FROM OUR BED. "WHAT'S THAT?" I ASK AS HE SHOVES SOMETHING INTO HIS POCKET.

"JUST A LITTLE SOMETHING I NEEDED."

"WHAT?" I ASK.

"NOTHING THAT CONCERNS YOU, EVY."

MY PET NAME WAS NOT GOING TO GET HEM OFF THE HOOK. WHATEVER, WHERE'S THE MONEY FROM YOUR CHECK? I'LL JUST USE —" AND IN THAT MOMENT IS WHERE IT ALL BLEW UP IN MY FACE. IN A SPLIT SECOND, HE HAD ME PINNED AGAINST THE WALL BY MY THROAT.

"DAMN IT EVELYN, I FUCKING ASKED YOU TO LET IT GO NOW LET IT THE FUCK GO. THERE AIN'T NO DAMN MONEY I GOT FIRED."

FROM MY BUSTED SWOLLEN LIP, I WATCH THE PINK TINTED WATER SWIRL DOWN THE SHOWERS DRAIN.

MORE

NOT NECESSARILY WORRYING ABOUT MY LIP, BUT RATHER, OUR INCOME. NO MONEY? FIRED? WHAT COULD HE HAVE POSSIBLY SPENT OUR LAST DOLLARS ON? I DO NOT BLAME HIM FOR HIS OUTBURST, HE OBVIOUSLY WAS UPSET OVER LOSING HIS JOB AND WAS JUST VENTING. BUT, HOW? WHY, DID HE LOSE HIS JOB? I PONDER ON ALL OF THIS, AND THEN IT HITS ME. WHAT WAS HE HIDING FROM ME? HE MUST HAVE PLAYED THE LOTTERY WITH THE LAST OF OUR MONEY AND DIDN'T WANT ME GETTING OVERZEALOUS.

DRIED OFF, I WRAP MYSELF IN A TOWEL AND PREPARE TO APOLOGIZE FOR NOT TRUSTING IN HIS ABILITY TO SUPPORT OUR FAMILY. WHEN I WALKED INTO OUR BEDROOM THOUGH, NOTHING COULD HAVE PREPARED ME FOR WHAT LAID BEFORE ME. MY HUSBAND PASSED OUT ON OUR BED WITH A NEEDLE PROTRUDING OUT OF HIS ARM.

CHAPTER 23

EVERYONE HAS A LIMIT, TO WHERE THEY KNOW, ENOUGH, IS ENOUGH. WELL, AT THE SIGHT OF HIM SHOOTING UP, SHOT ME WAY PAST THAT LIMIT AND ROCKETED MS OUT THE DOOR. I WAS SO FED UP AND ANGRY THAT I DIDN'T HAVE ANY PLANS WHATSOEVER. I JUST HAD TO GET OUT OF THERE AND OUT OF THAT ROOM, THAT HOUSE, THAT MARRIAGE. IT JUST ALL BECAME TOO MUCH. I KNOW WE SPOKE SOLEMN VOWS, WHICH INCLUDED "UNTIL DEATH DO US PART", YET OUR MARRIAGE, OUR RELATIONSHIP PERIOD, HAD BEEN SICK FOR A LONG TIME. SEEING THAT NEEDLE IN HIS ARM, TOOK HIM FROM ME.

NOW, I KNOW WHAT YOU MUST BE THINKING, "EVELYN, WHAT ABOUT YOUR THREE CHILDREN? YOU JUST LEFT THEM IN THAT TYPE OF ENVIRONMENT, WITH A FATHER WHO'S STRUNG OUT? NO HOUSEHOLD INCOME,

NO POSITIVITY TO SPEAK OF?" YES, ALL OF THAT IS TRUE, BUT FROM MY PERSPECTIVE, ON THAT DAY, WHEN I MADE MY DECISION TO LEAVE, IT WAS NEVER TO LEAVE THEM IN THAT PREDICAMENT INDEFINITELY. THE FRIDGE AND CUPBOARDS WERE STOCKED WITH ENOUGH FOOD FOR TWO WEEKS. DURING WHICH TIME, I WOULD ESTABLISH A PLACE FOR US TO STAY AND SOME SORT OF INCOME TO SUSTAIN US. IT WOULD HAVE BEEN EVEN MORE DIFFICULT FOR ME TO 0BTAIN THESE THINGS WITH THEM.

COULD I HAVE DONE THESE THINGS WITH THEM IN TOW? YES, BUT I'D RATHER THEM HAVE A ROOF OVER THEIR HEAD AND FOOD TO EAT FOR THE TIME BEING AS I SEARCHED, RATHER THAN HAVE THE STRESS OF HANGING IN LIMBO ABOUT OUR NEXT MEAL, OR WHERE WE WERE TO SLEEP. AS LIFE WOULD TAKE ITS COURSE, PLANS DON'T ALWAYS WORK OUT AS YOU SEE FIT.

I HAD FINALLY STUMBLED INTO A WOMANS SHELTER WHO SOON SET ME UP WITH AN INTERVIEW.

WITH A PROSPECTIVE EMPLOYER AND A HOME PLAN, TWO WEEKS TURNED INTO TWO MONTHS, LEAVING ME DEEPLY DEPRESSED. A SISTER FROM THE CHURCH OFFERED ME A POSITION OF VOLUNTEER WORK TO, IN THE LEAST, KEEP ME BUSY. "BLESSINGS COME TO THOSE WHO BLESS OTHERS," SHE USED TO TELL ME.

"BLESSINGS COME IN MANY FORMS." SISTER ANGELA HAD ONCE INFORMED ME. A BLESSING I WAS NOT EXPECTING, AND ONE I DIDN'T WANT, NOR READY FOR AT THE TIME. WOMEN WHO WERE WITH CHILD GOT PRIORITY.

NEARLY IN MY SECOND TRIMESTER, I RECEIVED A MANAGEABLE CLEANING JOB OF AN OFFICE BUILDING WORKING THE GRAVEYARD SHIFT, ALONG WITH A QUAINT STUDIO APARTMENT. WITH LITERAL POCKET CHANGE AFTER RENT AND BILLS WERE PAID, I WAS FORTUNATE ENOUGH TO RECEIVE DONATED FURNITURE. THE CHURCH ALSO DONATED CLOTHING FOR MY UNBORN CHILD AND I, WHILE ALSO OFFERING, AS LONG

AS I CONTINUED TO VOLUNTEER MY TIME, I COULD STILL HAVE MEALS AND FREE CHILDCARE, AT THE CHURCH.

I CONTINUED ON, ALAS, I HAD NO OTHER OPTION BUT TO. TOWARDS THE END OF MY PREGNANCY, I WAS OFFERED A SPOT ON THE CHURCHES NEW PROGRAM THEY WERE STARTING, A FEDERALLY GRANTED PROGRAM TO EDUCATE SINGLE MOTHERS. I WOULD HAVE TO ATTEND COLLEGE AND MAINTAIN AN AVERAGE OF AT LEAST 3.0 GPA. GETTING AN OPTION OF MEDICAL (CNA), HOSPITALITY, OR BUSINESS, I WAS EXCITED, NERVOUS AND ANXIOUS, ALL AT THE SAME TIME. BARELY SURVIVING AS I STOOD, MY FIRST REACTION WAS TO ACCEPT IT WHOLEHEARTEDLY, BUT ON THE TIME SCALE OF GETTING MY KIDS BACK, IT WOULD BE DELAYED CONSIDERABLY. IN THE LONG RUN, I THOUGHT, I WOULD BE BETTER ABLE TO PROVIDE FOR THEM.

JUNE 30TH, 1995, I GAVE BIRTH TO MY FINAL CHILD, A BOY. WHEN IT CAME TIME TO FILL OUT THE OFFICIAL DOCUMENTS, I WAS AT A LOSS: NAME OF MOTHER, NAME

OF FATHER, AND NAME OF CHILD. IN THE ASPECT OF MY NAME, I DEBATED WHETHER OR NOT, TO USE MY MAIDEN NAME, SINCE I WAS NOT YET DIVORCED FROM MY HUSBAND. AS FAR AS THE CHILDS NAME, I CAME UP WITH CHRISTOPHER, YET THE SAME ISSUE OF THE LAST NAME.

"BUT WAIT!" I THOUGHT. I HAD PUSHED IT SO FAR BACK INTO THE RECESS OF MY MIND THAT I HAVEN'T EVEN GIVEN ANY THOUGHT TO IT. THE TIME I CONCEIVED CHRISTOPHER, I HAD HAD SEX WITH TWO MEN IN THE COURSE OF TWENTY-FOUR HOURS. HOW COULD I POSSIBLY KNOW WHO HIS FATHER IS?

CHAPTER 24

"NOW, AS I LOOK AROUND, YOU'RE ALL MIRRORING MY SHOCK AND AWE, JUST BEFORE I WALKED OUT. AS I AM COVERING DR. GREGOR'S CASE LOAD, ALL I

MORE

WAS TOLD, BEFORE RECEIVING, WAS THAT THE PATIENT WAS IN A COMA. LIFTING MY HEAD FROM YOUR CHARTS AND INTO YOUR FACE, IT WAS TOO MUCH TO BEAR; LIKE LOOKING INTO A MIRROR.

"I MUST BE MISSING SOMETHING HERE," SALEEM SAYS. "SOMETHING'S NOT ADDING UP."

"NO, IT CAN'T BE. IT'S NOT POSSIBLE," I EXCLAIM FEELING MY BODY GO NUMB.

NOTICING MY REACTION, SALEEM GRABS MY HAND, "YANI, WHAT'S WRONG?"

I TURN TO CHRIS, "PLEASE TELL ME THIS ISN'T HAPPENING. PLEASE TELL ME THAT SHE IS LYING."

"I WISH I COULD BABY," HE RESPONDS,"BUT I ACTUALLY NEVER MET C-NOTE'S MOTHER."

"WAIT, WAIT. WHAT?!" SALEEM TURNS TO THE DOCTOR AND DEMANDS TO SEE HER ID. SURE ENOUGH, IT

MORE

INDICATED HER NAME AS DR. EVEYLYN COOPERFIELD.

"SO WHAT YOU ARE TELLING US IS..."

DR. COPPERFIELD FINISHES FOR HIM, "I CHANGED MY LAST NAME BACK TO MY MAIDEN NAME, WHICH I GAVE MY YOUNGEST SON, YOUR LITTLE BROTHER. WHO IN TURN, REPEATEDLY RAPED AND IMPREGNATED MY DAUGHTER, HIS SISTER WITH AN INCEST CHILD. FINALLY, IN KILLING HIM FOR KILLING KUERON, AND ALL HE HAS DONE TO YOUR SISTER, KILLED YOUR YOUNGER BROTHER.

EPILOGUE

TRAGEDY HAS BEFALLEN OUR LIVES, ONE NEVER TO BE IMAGINED, YET ONE NOT AS EASILY FORGOTTEN. NIGHTMARES HAVE TAKEN OVER ANY TIME I TRY TO SLEEP. LITTLE SLEEP CHRIS HAS GOTTEN SINCE I WAS RELEASED FROM THE HOSPITAL, NEVER LEAVING MY

SIDE. SALEEM HAS BEEM SO DEVASTATED OVER IT ALL,

THAT HE RARELY LEAVES HIS APARTMENT, LET ALONE

SPEAK TO ANYONE. YET, THE ONE THING WE ALL HAVE IN

COMMON, BESIDES EACH OTHER, IS WHERE TO PLACE THE

BLAME.

A SUCCESSFUL CAREER, A MORTGAGE FREE HOME,

THE THREE OF US HAVE THE, SAME QUESTION, "WHY

HASN'T EVEYLYN COME TO US SOONER?" RAW WITH

EMOTION, WE ARE IN FEAR OF ADDING SALT TO OUR

ALREADY GAPING WOUNDS WITH LIES AND EXCUSES. I,

FOR ONE, FIND MYSELF NOT TO ABLE TO COMMUNICATE

WITH HER. SHE HAS EXTENDED HER HAND NUMEROUS OF

TIMES. ALL I WANTED TO DO WAS CUT IT OFF.

LUNCHES, DINNERS, GIFTS: MONETARY AND

OTHERWISE; ALL OF WHICH I HAVE NO INTEREST IN. ALL I

KEEP THINKING ABOUT IS HOW I WANTED MY MOTHER

BACK INTO MY LIFE, NOW THAT I HAVE THAT

OPPORTUNITY, I KEEP REMEMBERING ALL OF THE PAIN,

ANGER AND STRIFE SHE CONTRIBUTED TO WHEN I DIDN'T

MORE

KNOW HER. IN THE LEAST, HER ACTIONS HAS BEEN NOTABLE.

SHE HAS BEEN TAKING CARE OF, AND REHABILITATING MY FATHER WHICH I CANNOT BRING MYSELF TO THANK HER, SIMPLY BECAUSE IN PART, SHE IS TO BLAME. I KNOW THAT SHE DID NOT INITIALLY STICK HIM IN THE ARM WITH THAT

NEEDLE, BUT SHE MAY AS WELL PRESSED THE SYRINGE, INJECTING HIS BODY WITH THE DRUGS, THE MOMENT SHE WALKED OUT OF THAT DOOR. SADNESS, ANGER, HATRED AND BITTERNESS ARE ALL I CAN EMOTE TOWARDS HER. OUR FAMILY TORN APART BY THOSE WITHIN, OF ITS' OWN PAIN, AND DEVASTATION. IS THERE ANY LIGHT IN SIGHT?

THE END

MORE